The Neon Owl

Book 1: When the Shit Hits the Van

by

Chad Lutzke

To join my VIP reader list and be included in all future
giveaways, visit www.chadlutzke.com
To become a patron and receive exclusive content, visit
www.patreon.com/ChadLutzke

Dedicated to Los Angeles.
We've never met, but I think you'd like me.

Introduction

A quick note about why it says "Book 1" on the cover. This book is a stand-alone. There's closure here, as is the case with each of The Neon Owl books. There will be no cliffhangers baiting you into the next one.

If you happen to read the books out of order, that's fine. You'll miss a little backstory but not enough to alienate you. The book order on the cover is for people like me. The completists. Those who want to make sure they start at the beginning. Not all books in a series list their order, so I'm saving you the time of hunting down publication dates.

That's it. There's your introduction. Now, get comfortable and find out how it all began.

Chapter 1: I Had Coltrane

The last relationship I was in ended the same way it started: me in pain. I'd caught my junk in my zipper, just a bit of skin, but enough to make me howl and take my sweet time zipping up ever since. The girl laughed her ass off, hurrying with her bra and struggling with the fasten. I didn't help. I'd lost all interest in chivalry. Her laugh was a sign of things to come. We lasted four months.

She was one of several that never worked out, and just another reason to leave Tacoma, the phone call from a lawyer being the catalyst.

"Your Aunt Ruth is dead, and she left you everything."

That's a direct quote. No bedside manner. No other details. And if I'd been closer to Aunt Ruth, I might have spit shit in his ear about breaking things gently. But I was too stunned.

Aunt Ruth didn't have a lot of money. It was all tied up in her motel, a shithole on Sunset Boulevard in West L.A. When I met with the lawyer, he showed me a photo that was at least twenty years old. And since time heals a building like nails fix a flat, I knew not to expect much once I got there.

"One stipulation," he'd said. "You can't sell it."

Aunt Ruth was adamant about the building staying in the family—me being the last in a short line. Unless, of course, there was a mini-me out there, and I can think of two incidents where that could be the case. The first was a hot little Mexican in Denver who frequented my bed for the better part of a week, just before I'd moved to Tacoma, a young lady who assured me The Pill had blocked any chance of our reproducing. It wasn't until after I'd moved that a friend shared the truth. She was no 20-year-old Judo instructor, but a 16-year-old high-school dropout. And before you go thinking ill of me, I was 17 at the time. This was no cradle robbing.

I've questioned the truth behind the pill ever since.

The other was a one-night stand. Your average drunken romp, most of which I couldn't remember, even if threatened with bamboo under my nails, except for one awkward moment. That trip a man takes to the bathroom after coitus? The one where he disrobes his johnson of its latex? Well, it was already gone. Eaten by a flower I'd never see

6

again. That's the one that worried me most. But I'm not the kind of guy to reject an unexpected knock on the door from a 17-year-old who has my eyes. I'd welcome it.

Anyway, the motel was mine now.

It took me less than a week to pack and tie loose ends, which included finishing the final 30 frames in my bowling league. We placed second and left with a trophy—one I promptly took to Goodwill, along with a bag of old clothes. I can't very well call myself a minimalist if I'm lugging around dust collectors like that. A trophy or a decorative vase, they're the same to me. Winning the trophy was nice, but I've got my mind to keep the memory.

So, four days later, I was there on the highway, pissing on the side of the road in the middle of a long drive to The City of Angels. I zipped up (slowly), took my last breath of fresh Washington air, then headed toward the van and rented trailer.

Everything I owned was in there. My collection of vinyl, the shelves to put them on, a turntable and speakers. I'm a minimalist, not soulless. A man without music is a man without. Period.

About minimalism, it doesn't always go hand in hand with that hippie, free-spirit bullshit. At least not for me. I'm no barefoot-trekking, weed-puffing, aging flower child who thinks the sun shines out of Jerry Garcia's ass. But my custom Dodge van puts me in that category for some: shag carpet, bed, mini-fridge, and a stereo system that'll turn heads three blocks away. But there's no wizard airbrushed on the side. No large-breasted barbarian. No dragons. Just a two-tone orange and purple that in the right light you'd swear had stars living on her.

When I left for L.A., I still hadn't named her. She deserved one, but nothing struck me as worthy. A woman's name didn't seem right, not with my lady luck. But as I ate the last stretch of highway, the sweet tenor of John Coltrane as my soundtrack, the name seemed obvious.

Gandalf had Shadowfax. B.B. had Lucille. And I had Coltrane.

Chapter 2: The Neon Owl

I'd been to L.A. once before. It was the 80s. Punk was dying, and the cock rock scene in full bloom, particularly around Sunset. Aqua Net and split ends for miles. Walk down the strip with an open flame and you were liable to light the whole street afire.

Mom and I had gone there to visit Aunt Ruth. This was pre-motel. Aunt Ruth had a husband then who owned real estate. But he wasn't my uncle. He was never awarded that title. This was her third husband, and not her last. I've forgotten his name, but I remember him being responsible for the change in Aunt Ruth. She went full-blown hippie. I'm talking meditation, yoga, tapestries, and a considerable amount of weed to keep it all tied together, keep the fog rollin'. She even changed her name to Luna Moon. Not legally, but it's who she was anymore. Mom refused to call her that, and I don't think the words crossed her lips once other than to poke fun.

This time, L.A. seemed busier somehow. More cars. More smog. More yoga mats and lemon water. I chalked up the change to perspective. Being older now, my eyes weren't zeroed in on tits and palm trees but on making my way down the 5 without dinging a bumper, while the drivers around me took glances at their cellphones, a Bluetooth stuck in their ears.

I took a detour down Livonia Avenue, drove by my aunt's old house. It'd been painted a different color, but the trees out front were the same, one of which I'd spent several hours in as a kid after catching a glimpse of bra through a window across the street. My cursed puberty kept me in that tree most of the day, hoping for just one more peek. Kids are perverted little creeps.

***

The motel was on the corner of Sunset Boulevard and Hamilton. Pink and blue, like stucco cotton candy. Overall, it was in decent shape, though I'd soon learn it was no longer a motel but a U-shaped strip of efficiency apartments. When Aunt Ruth bought it, she kept the name, as well as that godawful color scheme, and turned it into tiny apartments. Actually, the place was well kept. Evergreen hedges trimmed, the walkways free of weeds, and the sign out front lit up as it should—The Neon Owl.

I parked Coltrane in the back and locked her up, then headed toward the office, owner's keys in hand.

"Five bucks and I'll look after your van, make sure nobody messes with it." A thin man with skin like a saddle that's seen too much ass sat in between two hedges, his eyes ocean blue against the dark leather, his hair a halo of wild, thinning gray. I gave him a once over and asked if he lived here.

He patted the ground where he sat. "It's one of my spots. I make rounds so's I don't attract attention."

"You sleep out here?"

"Some nights. And some nights I'm down at the park. It gets crowded down there, so most the time I'm right here. Just don't tell Luna. She'll chase me away. She thinks I'm the one shittin' out here. But I'm not. That's Evan. I've seen him do it. Drop trou right in the bushes, like it's some kinda litter box. Luna don't believe me, though. She swears it's me. I said to her, *why would I shit where I sleep*? She don't wanna hear logic. Stubborn old woman."

"Luna passed away."

He wrinkled the leather around his eyes. "Well...that explains why I ain't seen her around. Who are you then?"

"I'm her nephew."

"She leave you The Owl?"

"That she did. You're not gonna be a problem are ya?"

"Oh, hell no. I mind my business. Now, how about that five bucks?"

"I'm not paying you to watch the van."

"Well, then don't come crying to me if—"

"You'll be the first I come to."

"I see how it is."

"Good."

I walked away and the man followed.

"Hold up. How 'bout five bucks just for the hell of it?"

"You *are* gonna be a problem, aren't ya?"

"Hey, a man's gotta make a living."

"What are you gonna spend it on?"

"Gonna get drunk."

I appreciated the honesty and pulled some bills from my pocket. "Here's three. You'll have to settle for Wild Irish or Mad Dog."

"Aww, hell."

"Don't puke in the bushes. And don't shit in them either."

"I done told you—"

"Yeah, we'll see."

The guy shuffled away while I unlocked the office and hit the light. The first thing I saw was a computer sitting on a desk behind the counter. The damn thing sent a spike through my gut.

Because of Audrey.

Audrey was the one who got away. It was a full two years of bliss, which is no kind of record, but it's the one that hurt the most because it didn't have to end. A dream-job opportunity popped up, swept her away, and I loved her too much to hinder it. The worst part was not following her. Guess which smog-filled city she moved to. Yep. Last I knew, she was still here. Last I knew, she was single. But last I knew was four years ago. That computer at the desk was a temptress. If I wanted to find Audrey, that'd be my source, and it'd probably only be a matter of time before I sought her out, see if those embers still burned.

The lawyer had spoken of a notebook in the desk at the office, said there were instructions in it. He told me every year for the last four Aunt Ruth would update it. He said she liked being organized, which included every detail regarding her funeral, burial, and will. She never wanted to be a burden on anyone, especially from the grave. It was a whole lot of premeditation for someone who wasn't sick, but she died how we'd all like to: in her sleep.

I found the notebook, flipped past pages that'd been crossed out, then found the beginning of Aunt Ruth's updated instructions. There were two names listed— both of them residents she'd hired. And as a posthumous favor to her, she wanted it kept that way, for them to keep their respective duties as well as their beds. I had no problem with that.

Anne was to clean any recently vacated apartments. Aunt Ruth stressed the importance of keeping her on, as she was the single mother of two young boys.

Roddy was the handyman, an all-purpose guy. He was paid a small salary and stayed rent-free. He was the first I met later that night, drunk as can be and with only a single leg to stand on.

Chapter 3: Roddy

Roddy knocked on the office door close to 10:00 p.m. I was still going through the office, looking for everything that'd help me in the transition from blue-collar to business owner.

Roddy looked to be in his late 50s, early 60s. He wore a ballcap with shaggy gray poking out around his ears and a T-shirt hidden under a polyester, short-sleeved button-up covered in a duck print. When I opened the door, he hit me with breath that could have wilted flowers—an alcohol-fueled wind carrying the last meal he'd had.

"Hello. I'm Roddy. I'm the maintenance guy 'round here. Live over in apartment three...no, four. The one with the red light over the door...whatever the hell. You mush be Jinx."

"Hi, Roddy. Nice to meet you. Just getting settled in."

"Good, good." Roddy looked past me into the office, like he was taking in one last peek at familiar surroundings before they changed.

"How can I help you?"

"Ohhh...I thought I'd jush introduce me to you."

I invited him in, and he hopped on his one leg around the counter and to the back of the office, took a seat. He wore a pair of jeans, half of which were cut-offs, his stump jutting out just past the denim fringe which hung like ghostly tendrils.

The office and Aunt Ruth's apartment were conjoined by a single door, her apartment being twice as big as the others—two separate efficiencies with the wall removed, making for a decent-sized studio suite.

"So, how long have you lived here, Roddy?"

"Some would say too long. I first shtepped through that door," he pointed toward the office door. "March 31st, 1988, and the woman behind the counter there, your Aunt Luna, she took my breath away. I tried to charm her, get shomethin' goin', but she never bit.

"Eighty-eight? That's a helluva long stay."

"Used to think about her when I jerked the johnson. She was a real beauty queen."

"I'm probably not the best ear for confessions like that."

"Sorry, young man. Some would shay that's too much information. You'll have to forgive me. I'm not really a drinker, but the loss of Luna has got me all flubbed up."

Roddy stared at the floor like there was a whole ocean of something to look at, then shook his head.

"So, when you're on the job, you're sober, right?"

He sat up so straight I thought he might salute me. "Jinx...I ain't never drank in my life until a week ago."

"Never?"

"Not unless you count the tit-milk from the boozer who birthed me."

"Roddy, I think I like you. But I wanna meet you in better spirits. How about you get home, get some sleep, and in the morning we'll see if we can't find you something broke that needs fixing."

"You got it, Jinx." He stood up on his one leg, hopped back around the counter and to the door, then swiveled back. "I don't suppose you got a picture of Luna maybe you would part with?"

I thought about how I'd be giving a stranger a picture of my aunt that, based upon his earlier confession, would most likely be used for some grieving masturbation. I told him I didn't, but he was welcome to one of the paintings on the wall since I'd be taking them down anyway.

He smiled and hopped toward a wall lined with paintings, every one of them an owl. He took one, thanked me, and hopped out the door and back home to apartment three. Or four.

***

I lugged in 3,000-plus records, the shelves, turntable and speakers from the trailer. Not quite unpacked but settled enough. I hooked up the stereo and drew blindly from a box of vinyl—Dave Brubeck—then spun the sweet sounds of *Nightshift* while I broke into a six-pack I'd brought with me. I'm not big on drinking—the pack would last me a week—but I like to lighten up when the day calls for it. And after a long drive and moving all that vinyl, the day called for it.

From my experience so far at The Owl, alcohol seemed to be a common denominator among the locals, and I hoped Roddy wasn't pulling my leg about not being a drunk himself. It wasn't in my plans to babysit the inebriated.

I found a clean set of sheets and pillowcase in the closet, stripped the bed, then downed the beer and let Brubeck ease me to sleep.

Chapter 4: Suspects

I woke with the thought of Aunt Ruth breathing her last on that very mattress and decided to swap it for another in storage. Storage was apartment #12, used solely for the purpose of holding cleaning supplies, mattresses, linen, light bulbs, and Roddy's tools. Buying a new mattress wasn't an option. I had *some* savings, but not much, and Aunt Ruth had very little money. So, I'd need to pinch pennies until I figured out just how much The Owl brought in, and how much went out. There were also taxes to consider and an emergency fund for the unexpected.

Thankfully, Aunt Ruth's cupboards were stocked with plenty of food, though every bit of it vegan. I've had worse. I lived off canned tuna and peanut butter sandwiches for an entire summer, with nothing but grapefruit juice to wash them down. At least here there was variety: soups, kale chips, rice, beans, cereals, vegetables, pasta, potatoes, and even imitation bacon bits. With a well-populated spice rack and a bit of imagination, I could do a whole lot with what was available, though springing for a block of Velveeta would put a little bit of Heaven into every one of those dishes. I put cheese at the top of my to-do list.

There was no coffee—Aunt Ruth was a tea drinker—so, I added that to the list as well and made plans to hit the store after breakfast. I'd barely gotten out of the shower when there was a knock at the office door. It was 8:00 a.m.

Roddy stood outside with a cup of coffee and a bright, smiling face that lacked the red, glassy eyes from the night before.

"Good morning, Roddy."

'Mornin'. Got a minute?"

"Was about to eat breakfast. I suppose you could join me."

"Don't mind if I do. Luna leave any of them Grape Nuts?"

"Think I saw a box in there."

We ate bowls of Grape Nuts drowned in honey and soymilk, and slices of toast with the worst *butter* I'd ever had. I added milk and butter to the list.

"You remember anything from last night?" I asked.

"All too well, unfortunately. Sorry about that." He took a bite of toast, and I could see he didn't care much for the butter either. "Thanks for the painting. Hung it up this morning."

"You can take 'em all if you want."

"You should leave at least one. It's The Owl, after all."

"I suppose that makes sense."

Roddy caught me catching a glimpse of his leg and started in on its origin.

"It's an embarrassing story, but you may get a kick out of it. I was eighteen, out with friends, looking for some mud for my turtle, and there was this beautiful young gal whose name escapes me, which makes the whole thing even worse. But I was tryin' to impress her that night, and while we was out by an alligator farm after hours...well, I hopped the fence and landed right on the bastard's head. You can figure out the rest. Needless to say, I didn't get laid that night." He chuckled at the thought, and you could see in his face it wasn't something he let bother him anymore. "How 'bout yourself? Any that got away on account of stupidity?"

I thought of Audrey and wondered if it was stupid not to chase after, relocate along with her. She'd made the suggestion, but instead I wallowed in Tacoma, pretending she was just another fish, not knowing I'd still be rubbing that bruise four years later.

"I'm afraid you've got me beat, Roddy."

***

After breakfast, we headed outside. Roddy wanted to give me a tour of the place. The moment we walked into the L.A. morning air, I smelled shit. Human shit.

Roddy smelled it, too. "That'd be Charlie," he said.

"That's the third person now I'm hearing might be shittin' in the bushes."

"Who else you got?"

I told him about meeting Bush-Guy the night before and how Aunt Ruth had blamed him, but he blamed a guy named Evan. Roddy told me Bush-Guy's name was Wayne and how Aunt Ruth didn't care much for him. Not just because she was convinced he was using the bushes to do his business, but because she'd seen him peeking in her window one night.

"Hmm. So, we've got ourselves three suspects," Roddy said.

Suspects. Hearing the word stirred something in me I hadn't felt in a long time. Growing up, I dreamt of being a cop. Well, not so much a cop as a detective. Even if it meant never hitting the street but working on the case right at a desk, scouring case files and putting two and two together.

By the time I hit 20, I'd enrolled in police academy. I lasted eight weeks before dropping out. My killing that dream was a mixture of things. I was in a strange headspace at the time, floating between knowing exactly what I wanted and not having a clue. I was also having a passionate love affair with weed. Weed and motivation go together like oil and water.

But most of all, I realized my childhood dream of solving cases would first include a decade or two of handing out tickets, showing up at car accidents and mediating domestic disputes, all while wearing a cumbersome belt. There would be no trench coat, no flipping my credentials from a thin, leather wallet. So, I quit, stayed in a cannabis fog for the next two years, and got a mindless job digging holes.

That day at The Owl, it seemed silly getting excited about a mystery shitter, figuring out who was dumping alongside an old motel. But dammit if I wasn't up for putting the clues together.

***

Roddy and I killed two birds. While showing me around, pointing out who lives where and flavoring each name with a bit of gossip, we found the culprit turd mashed into the ground between the same hedges I'd spotted Bush-Guy Wayne the night before. My first thought was maybe Wayne was telling the truth. Sure didn't make sense to dump where you sleep. I asked Roddy about Evan and what he looked like, what his story was.

"Just another poor S.O.B. lookin' for a place to lay his head. City's full of 'em."

He told me Evan always wore a yellow ball cap with the bill ripped off, said he didn't know if that was a fashion statement or the only thing he had to keep the sun off his scalp.

Roddy offered to dispose of the feces with a pail and shovel, then went and fetched them and tossed the shit in the dumpster.

"Jinx, you may wanna see this." Roddy stood leaning against the dumpster on his one leg, a red pail in his hand. I didn't tell him he looked like a broken lawn jockey.

I peeked in the dumpster, and inside was a collection of turds, one for nearly every day of the week. I asked Roddy if it was possible he put the mess in there after cleaning out the bushes during his week-long bender.

"That's not the kind of thing you forget. Hell, first turd I've picked up was just now. Either Luna took care of 'em or someone else did."

I asked why he thought this Charlie guy was guilty, and Roddy said because of how the man smelled. "It's like he's still wearing the first diaper his momma ever gave him."

When I asked for a description of Charlie, he said I didn't need one, that I'd smell him before I ever saw him. "…But he's got a moustache, one of them thin ones, all greased down. And long hair he keeps tucked under one of them Panama hats, all dirty. He's a foul mess, I'm tellin' you."

I swear I picked up on a little of his own excitement about getting to the bottom of things, and after scratching our heads for a few near the dumpster, Roddy went home, and I left for the store in search of cheese, coffee, milk, and butter.

Chapter 5: Tea-Time Tuesday

I wasn't sure Audrey still lived in L.A., but it was a good assumption. If you're going to up and leave one life to start another, that next stop is usually a permanent one. The idea she could be so close kept her on my mind more than usual.

I'd yet to turn the computer on. It was an intimidating beast—skull-white in color with a beady, red eye that seemed to follow each time I passed it. I didn't know shit about computers.

When I was at the store, I got myself a little notebook, the kind that fits in the palm of your hand with the spiral on top instead of the side. The kind a detective might use, hurriedly flipping it open when questioning witnesses during an investigation.

On the first page, I wrote the three "suspects" names: Wayne, Charlie, Evan, with a brief description of each, then tossed it on the desk and made a grilled cheese. I sat in my apartment, ate, and thought about unpacking. It'd feel a lot more like home with my records on the shelves.

That's when the office door rang, and the unmistakable scent of human feces filled the room. Roddy was right. I smelled him before I even saw him.

Charlie stood at the counter with darting eyes and itching fingers. He reminded me a bit of Smeagol, but with a mustache and better posture. The chronic itching was similar to that of someone with a chemical dependency, though I couldn't be sure that was the case.

"How can I help you?"

The man set a giant coffee mug on the counter and said, "It's tea-time Tuesday. I...I missed last week." The mug was big enough to hold a can of soup, maybe more.

"Sorry, buddy. I don't follow."

He looked at his wrist as if he sported a watch instead of thick, black hair hiding dirty skin. "It's...it's Tuesday, right?"

"I'm new here, so you'll have to spell it out for me."

"The lady...she gives me tea on Tuesdays. But...but I missed last week."

It dawned on me just how many people depended on Aunt Ruth, be it for employment, a place to crash, or a weekly beverage of unusually significant importance. Without giving details, I broke the news that Aunt Ruth no longer ran The Owl.

"She doesn't work here anymore, but I might be able to hook you up. I don't know about every Tuesday, though."

The guy looked at me liked I'd just run over his cat.

"No more tea-time Tuesday?"

"Let's just get through today, then worry about next Tuesday when it comes. Now, we talkin' iced or...?"

"Hot. Honey-lemon with ginger, twelve fluid ounces of tap water, and a straw."

The man's itching turned to the shakes while he hugged himself as though freezing.

"Okay, give me a minute."

I hurried to where'd I'd seen the tea before, and as I waited for the tap to get hot, I realized I had no idea where the ginger was or in what format. I'd only ever had ginger once. It was at a sushi bar with Audrey, and the tang stuck to my tongue for hours. I was so uneducated in the ways of ginger that I wasn't sure if Aunt Ruth grated it straight from the root, poured a drop of concentrate, or if it came in a shaker, like salt and pepper. Hell, I didn't even know if it was something you refrigerated.

"Just cut a slice off and put it in the bottom of the cup." Charlie said it like he knew my struggle.

I finally found the root in a small cupboard reserved for spices, cut a slice, filled the cup with water and dropped the ginger in.

"Dip the bag seven times please, then pinch it."

I did as instructed, then brought him the tea.

"Straw...please."

I searched for a straw, and once again he schooled me. "The silverware drawer." He was right.

When I gave him the straw, he dropped it in the tea and stirred it with trembling hands. He took a deep whiff of the tea, stuck his tongue in it, then flared his nostrils and sucked the whole cup down through the straw. By the time he was done, the shaking had stopped. No more twitching and itching, and there was a confidence in his voice that wasn't there before.

"Thank you, kind sir. Now, if you'll excuse me." And he walked out the door, empty mug in hand. The shit smell stayed.

I watched him walk down the road, made sure he didn't make a pit stop near the bushes. I made a note to pick up some second-hand clothes and give them to him next Tuesday.

***

I fired up the computer, pretending it was because I'm a business owner now and firing up computers is part of the job. I was prompted to put in a password, which Aunt Ruth left in her notes. A few seconds later, I'm staring at a desktop background—a smooth pile of stones stacked strategically on a beach, a sunset in the distance.

There were a few folders on the desktop: *Residents*, *Recipes*, *Tranquility*, and *Contacts*. I clicked on *Tranquility*. It was full of high-definition photos, much like the desktop background—landscapes, skyscapes, flower gardens, and shorelines. There were music files too, with titles like *Meditative Bliss* and *Soothing Soundscapes*.

I stayed away from the *Recipes* folder and went through *Residents*. It contained a spreadsheet of names, dates, security deposit amounts, rents due, and even little notes next to each tenant's name. Things like *"owns a parakeet," "deals pot,"* and *"poor girl."* I'd already heard the *"deals pot"* rumor from Roddy. Next to Roddy's name it said, *"cute, able-bodied as they come."* I imagine Roddy would be hopping all up and down Sunset if he saw that. I decided to keep it a secret. He seemed to have found some closure, and I liked him sober.

I eyed the Internet browser, the cursor hovering over it.

The key to finding Audrey.

I waited for reasons to click, waited for reasons not to.

Click.

The fact I wasn't computer savvy was a blessing and a curse. Google stared back at me from the screen. I knew enough about it to use keywords. Enough to rip the wound open. I typed in Audrey's full name and went back to hovering and waiting.

I turned in the chair and looked through the doorway into my apartment—a neatly made bed surrounded by cardboard-box walls filled with clothes, vinyl, and not much else.

I closed the browser and turned off the screen.

Chapter 6: Crystal-Anne

Most of Aunt Ruth's things were packed, which I felt guilty about. I didn't know her that well and here she left me her entire life, which I boxed up like it all meant nothing. No tears shed, no moment of silence. And based on what I'd seen, I missed out on knowing someone pretty special. There's something to be said about not only mourning the loss of what you once had, but what you never had.

I lined the shelves against the wall and put my records away. Aunt Ruth had a nice reading chair in the corner I decided to keep, and I made plans to visit the library, get myself a card. I'm a one-book-at-a-time kind of guy, and you know my stance on clutter, which includes books. No sense in it. Besides, I love libraries. Places of solitude, surrounded by a billion words on a million pages. Let them hoard the books and I'll borrow them. One at a time. Keep things simple, clean, organized.

I dusted every inch of the place, washed the windows, too. The drapes would have to go. Enormous orange and white flowers against a forest-green background born right out of the 70s. I dig that era. Hell, look at Coltrane. But those drapes? That's not nostalgia. That's a horror show.

While dusting, I came across a group of polished stones on the windowsill next to the bed—some new-age stuff Aunt Ruth was into. For whatever reason, I left the stones there. A little area of remembrance for a woman I barely knew, but wished I had.

Everything I owned was in its place. The apartment had my stamp on it. The replacement mattress was kinder on my back, and it felt better knowing it wasn't a deathbed.

Later that night, I went for a walk. I saw Bush-Guy Wayne sleeping in his spot between the two hedges. Didn't have the heart to wake him. If he minded his business, and there were no complaints, I'd look the other way. He's not down-and-out by choice. Life has a way of kicking asses at random. Wayne could have been a real hero once. Maybe had a wife and kids. Something could have happened to them, sent him off the deep end. Maybe that wasn't his story, but he had one. And it was probably a heartbreaker.

The Owl was across the street from a titty bar called Paradise Island, which brought prostitutes. They took advantage of the blue ballers pouring out of the club, which didn't seem fair, like selling water in the desert. But these were businesswomen, with a business plan. They reminded me of spiders at a lake house. The land is full of them, spinning their webs in every nook and cranny because they know a lake brings a plethora of bugs. They know where to feast. Just like the hookers, spinning their own kind of webs, charging for a quick drink in the desert.

After my walk, I sat in the back of Coltrane, doors open and catching the breeze, beer in hand. I watched cars come and go across the street, girls being dropped off, girls being picked up. At 10:00 p.m., a woman came out the side door of the club. She crossed the street and headed straight for me, like she was on mission. The closer she got, the more I realized she meant to speak to me. And she did.

"You can't sell drugs here, so take your shop and get lost," she said.

"What? I'm not selling drugs. I'm having a beer and watching the strip."

"Looks like you're waiting on customers to me. Leave, or I'll call the police."

"Woah! Calm down, missy. I live here. This is my van. I'm just enjoying the night."

"Bullshit. You don't live here. I know every single person who does."

"Not only do I live here, but I own the place."

She stalled a moment, peeked in the back of the van, looked toward the office, then back at me. "You're the new guy?"

"Ruth was my aunt."

"Who the hell's Ruth?"

"Luna...Luna was my aunt."

"So, she left you The Owl?"

"Yep, just moved in."

The woman opened her purse all casual like, grabbed something from it, and pointed it at my face. It was pepper spray.

"Okay, what the hell!"

"Why'd you call her Ruth?"

"That's her name...her real name. Luna Moon is the hippie name she gave herself."

The woman seemed to consider my words. "Yeah, I can see that." She lowered the spray and took a seat next to me on the back of the van. "I'm Crystal...but you can call me Anne. I've got a fake name too, I guess. I live in apartment 10."

"Okay, that makes sense now. I suppose I should be grateful, you looking out for the place."

"I've got two kids in there. I don't want any drug shit going down in their backyard."

"Two kids? Ohh, you're the single mom who cleans the apartments."

"Yep. So, you got a name?"

"Sorry. Jinx." I extended my hand and she took it, gave a firm shake. Not like a man, but like a woman who doesn't take any shit.

"Jinx?" She had a beautiful smile, with dimples that didn't reveal themselves until then. "You've got a fake name too, huh?"

"Something like that. Had it since I was a kid, just kind of stuck."

"It's cute." Her face hardened after she said it. "That's not an invitation, so don't go poppin' a boner. You'll never touch these."

I couldn't help but laugh. She was strong as stone. Assertive and spunky.

"I suppose in order to get a peek at 'em all's I gotta do is walk through that red door over there before 10:00."

"I'd rather you didn't."

"Don't worry. That's not my thing. I like to earn my tits."

"Is that why you have this ridiculous van?"

"Ridiculous? Your ass was in it before you even knew my name."

"Shit...touché."

I asked her about the suspects.

"I may have seen them. But I see new faces on the strip every day and mind my own business, except when it comes to looking out for my babies. I'm just trying to save money and get the hell out of here, give them a better life."

"How old are they?"

"Eleven and eight."

"They home by themselves?"

"I've got no choice." She looked like she might cry. "They're good kids, though. You don't have to worry about them causing any trouble."

"No worries here."

"I should get home."

"Yeah, get your ass out of this ridiculous van."

The dimples came back.

"Nice meeting you."

"You too."

She went home while I drank the last bit of my beer.

"Don't listen to her, Coltrane. You're beautiful."

I walked back to the office, satisfied with my decision to move to L.A. The lights, the city life. It was everything I'd been missing. I locked up and headed to my apartment with that bastard computer watching me, doing what it could to pull me in.

"Not tonight, asshole."

With a city breeze climbing through the window, I slept deep. Then woke with the sun, and the smell of human shit.

Chapter 7: Minor Threat

I was standing over the mess, still in my boxers, hands on my hips, when I heard Roddy's unmistakable hop across the parking lot.

"I'm on it." He already had his shovel and pail. "I could tell by the look on your face you weren't lookin' at nothing but a turd."

"I wouldn't call it a turd so much as a puddle. We're gonna need the hose."

Roddy hopped over beside me, and we stared at it together like we were at a gallery and the brown on the ground was the next best thing in the art world, making interpretations on what the piece meant.

"Smells," Roddy said.

"Ya think?"

"I mean, that's straight from the bowels of hell right there. Downright demonic."

We sprayed the area, scattered the loose stool into the earth. I even sprinkled some carpet deodorizer.

"You know what we need to do? We need to catch the guy in the act," Roddy said.

That excitement stirred again. "A stakeout?"

"We'll take shifts, seeing how it happens in the small hours."

I told myself this was part of my responsibility as owner and operator of The Neon Owl, to keep the place clean, open, functioning, and free of assholes. I told myself that because the real reason I took to Roddy's suggestion was embarrassing. The young detective in me was doing cartwheels, like a giddy schoolgirl having been asked to prom.

Once back in the office, I fetched the little spiral notebook and flipped to the list of suspects. I sat at the desk and made a column labeled *Motive* after the names. I stared at it, studied each name. What the hell kind of motive does someone need to shit in the bushes, other than too much Mexican? You get a belly full of authentic, and you're ready to shit in your own hand if need be. But a serial defecator with a penchant for evergreens? I left the column blank.

I studied the notes I'd written the day before, put a face to each name, though I'd yet to meet Evan. That little fact could either raise suspicion or kill it altogether. Had I not seen him because he hadn't been around? Or because his visits were stealthy and nocturnal? And Charlie wore the cologne of the guilty. I made a note to question them all with some gentle interrogation.

I went back to bed, figured if I'm gonna be up all night I should be prepared. When you're thirty-plus, losing a full night of sleep is like running a marathon without moving. It's a whole different type of hangover. Out of sync with the world and still stuck in yesterday.

***

I woke around 10:30 a.m., made breakfast, and went over a spreadsheet Aunt Ruth had tacked to a board in the office. The sheet showed due dates for the rent of each tenant. She had a strange system. Apartment #2 was due yesterday. This was part of owning The Owl I wasn't looking forward to—knocking on doors and collecting late payment. Evicting I'd like even less.

With this kind of business, you need discernment. You need to be able to tell who's full of shit and who's on the level. Some people, they're born to take advantage of others, never taking responsibility, giving excuse after excuse. When it comes down to it, they're lazy and irresponsible. And others, they're legitimately going through a tough time, despite trying their best to make ends meet. It was my job to know the difference and make the appropriate call based on the reading.

I consider myself a good judge of character, able to put the clues together. It's like predicting the weather. Clouds mean rain, and you dress appropriately. You don't make picnic plans or head to the beach. If the tenant in apartment #2 answers the door with sunken eyes and scab-ridden arms, that's a storm coming.

The door opened after the first knock. This is where discernment begins. The tenant wasn't playing the avoidance game. That's a good sign. We've all played that game at some point. Whether it be hiding from the landlord, a schoolteacher, or your boss at work. In the case of landlords, you avoid the confrontation by not answering the door. Or if you're like my friend, Kev, you stage an elaborate lie. Because Kev's landlord would peek through his windows, Kev took to sleeping under his own bed, bedsprings an inch from his nose. He'd sneak out for work in the morning and wouldn't go home until midnight. He did that for two weeks. The finale was when he showed up at his landlord's in a borrowed wheelchair, apologizing for being late on rent but he'd been in the hospital. When the landlord pressed him for details, my friend pulled the trauma card: *'I'm not ready to talk about it.'* The landlord knocked two weeks off his rent. Conniving, but genius.

A young girl stood in the doorway, couldn't have been more than 16, 17 tops. I gave her a quick spiel about being the new owner of The Neon Owl and asked if a parent was around.

"I was afraid of this," the girl said.

"Afraid of what?"

She rolled her eyes and sighed. "My parents don't live here. I live by myself. Luna lets me stay. We had an agreement. And if that's not enough for you, then come in and maybe I can convince you."

I threw my hands up. "Woah! First of all, you're just a kid. I'm not about to...you know. Good lord...what the hell?"

"So, we cool then?"

"Hang on. What's the agreement? She let you live here for free? Because I can't—"

"Hell, no. I pay my way. She lets me stay even though I'm a minor. That's all."

"How old are you?"

"Sixteen."

"Where are your parents?"

She shrugged. "Probably dead."

"So, how long you been living here?"

"Ten months."

"And you work?"

"I pay my rent, if that's what you're worried about."

"One of a few things, yes, which is actually why I'm here."

"Shit...hang on."

She went inside, then came back and handed me a stack of bills.

"Can I ask where you work?"

"Yeah."

"But you're not gonna tell me."

"Listen, I'm a good tenant. I'm quiet. I pay my rent. I don't sell drugs or beg for booze money in the parking lot. That's all you should be worried about."

"If I were a heartless asshole, sure."

"Aww, how sweet." Full of sarcasm.

I counted the money she'd given me and handed half back to her. "This is how much your rent is from now on. Take the rest and save it, use it to get on your feet, get some clothes for a better job."

"I'm not a charity case."

"No, you're a young lady who I suspect hates your current job, and you're better than that."

I gathered it was the first time she'd been told something like that because her chin quivered and her eyes welled. Then she slammed the door in my face.

Roddy rolled into the parking lot as I was heading back to the office. He hopped out of his truck carrying two grocery bags.

"Need a hand with that?"

"I got it. I'm missin' a leg, not an arm."

"Speaking of which, that a stick you're drivin'?"

"Keeps me busy."

"I'll bet. That takes some talent."

"Not enough to bring the ladies."

Roddy leaned against his truck while he shut the driver door, then hopped around the back, opened the tailgate and took a seat on it, with the grocery bags next to him. "Got some supplies for the stakeout." He pulled out two thermoses and a pair of binoculars. "We'll need all the coffee we can get."

"Agreed, but why the thermoses? I got plenty of cups."

"I figured we'd camp out in that hippie van of yours, fill these up, piss in a 2 liter when nature calls, and keep ourselves hidden."

"Not bad. I got a bed in there. Whoever's on shift can sit in the front, the other crash in the back. But you really think we'll need these?" I held up the binoculars.

"I got a little excited. Don't need walkie talkies either, but if they had 'em I would have sprung for 'em."

We sat on the back of Roddy's truck and talked, watching lonely men walk through the red door across the street, pockets full of ones.

"Now, *that* I don't get," Roddy said. "Spots like that are a frustrating mess. Like going to a burger joint on an empty stomach and watching 'em cook, 'cept you can't order anything, and there ain't no food waitin' at home."

I watched Roddy swing his one leg over the tailgate like we were wading off a dock, and asked him about crutches, something I thought of the first time I saw him hopping around.

"I don't need no assistive device. I get around just fine."

"I can't tell if that's pride or stupidity."

"It's the truth."

"Well, you've never seen yourself hoppin' across the parking lot. I have."

"That bad, huh?"

"Worse." I smiled and patted Roddy on the back. My way of telling him, crutches or not, I liked him.

"I was thinkin' tonight we should park down the road. If this turd burglar comes and sees one of us sittin' in the van right here in the parking lot, he's liable to pinch it elsewhere. We'll have stayed up for nothin'."

"Good point."

"Then these would actually come in handy." Roddy lifted the binoculars to his eyes, looking off in the distance at a patch of dense trees down Hamilton behind The Owl. "Uh, Jinx...I think we can rule Evan out."

Roddy handed me the binoculars and I looked through them in the same direction he had. There in the middle of the trees was a man hanging upside down by his foot, somehow still sporting the yellow cap Roddy had told me about. The one with the missing bill. The guy wasn't moving, just hanging there, and from what I could tell, dead as can be.

Chapter 8: Eulogy

Just in case Evan still had life in him, we wasted no time getting there. I felt bad about leaving Roddy so far behind, pogoing like a rabbit on fire, but I had no choice, and maybe he'd see a pair of crutches wasn't a bad idea after all.

When I got to Evan, there was no question he was dead. The smell of rot not being the solidifying evidence, but the color of his face. With that yellow cap still stuck to him, his head was like a giant, ripe plum resting in a grapefruit halve—bloated and black as night where the blood had pooled.

Roddy finally made his way to me, and we stared up at Evan, thinking out loud on how it could have happened.

"Well," Roddy said. "That ain't no suicide."

"No murder either."

"Looks and smells like he's been here a while, so he's not our man. Besides, he was full when God took him." Roddy pointed out the bulge in the seat of Evan's pants.

Wrapped around Evan's leg was a rope that extended to the tree. It'd been used to tie an old vinyl tent to two branches. The other end was wrapped tight around his neck. We surmised Evan had made himself a hammock, gotten tangled in his sleep, and fell out of bed. If he didn't break his neck in the fall, I could see the poor guy kicking out with his foot, trying to break free but chokin' himself in the process. An embarrassing way to go.

"Should we say a few words?" I asked.

Roddy shrugged.

I thought on what to say, then cleared my throat and bowed my head. "Evan, I didn't know you, but...sorry you had to sleep in the trees and not in a real bed, around loved ones...and sorry for making you a suspect for something you didn't do." I raised my head and passed the torch to Roddy by way of a nod.

"I got nothin' to say. The guy was an asshole."

I looked back at Evan and told him to rest in peace.

We walked (and hopped) out of the smell and out of the trees and back to The Owl to call the police, confident we'd solved the puzzle on what could have happened.

"Was that your first body?" Roddy asked.

"In the wild? Yes. But I've seen my share at the hospital. Worked as a custodian when I was young. I'd mop the morgue floor every night, something they'd pawn off on the new guy. Most the time, bodies were in the coolers. But once in a while an examiner worked late and I'd catch a glimpse or two. How about yourself?"

"Twice. Kid I went to school with was stung by a bee. Took him out quick."

"And the other?"

"We'll save that for another time. Go make the call. I'll hang here. The cops will probably wanna talk to both of us."

I headed to the office where I'd left my cell, wondering if I'd just opened a wound Roddy just as soon leave closed.

***

The police showed ten minutes later, followed by an ambulance, and eventually a coroner in an unmarked van. A uniformed cop questioned us while they took pictures of Evan, then got him out of the tree, along with his makeshift hammock. The cop had a notebook just like mine, and took down our names and numbers, then wrote a few other things I couldn't make out. But not from lack of trying. The cop gave me a strange look and closed the notebook. It was like getting caught cheating on a test, looking over the shoulder of the kid in front of me.

"Well, looks like an open-and-shut case," the cop said. "Should we find any evidence of foul play, we'll be in touch." He was full of clichés, surprised he didn't squeeze *vic* in there somewhere. Probably wanted to be a detective too, sat at home on his days off watching *Columbo*. Hell, maybe I was jealous.

Roddy went to his place and ate while I hung around and watched them haul Evan away. Most the vehicles were parked on Hamilton and not in the parking lot at The Owl, which was good. I didn't want the tenants thinking someone had gotten murdered there. A small crowd gathered anyway, including a kid who looked straight out of Ridgemont High—long hair the color of piss, in nothing but a pair of flamingo-print shorts. I watched him as they loaded Evan into the coroner's van. He was in a puffy-eyed daze that held long after the van doors closed. I walked over to him and had a little fun at his expense.

"Got a hold of some bad reefer and thought he was a bird, jumped right out of that tree over there."

I could see the kid swallow hard with a cotton-dry throat. His jaw dropped a little. "Woah!" was all he could get out, then turned and walked toward The Owl, disappearing through the door of apartment #7.

Well, shit. There's our resident weed dealer.

Chapter 9: Regression

After lunch, I remembered a single picture of Audrey I kept in the side pocket of my backpack. As part of both healing and minimizing, I'd gotten rid of every photo of her except that one. I've heard it said you should never try and hold onto the past because it'll slow down your future, that you wouldn't live to your full potential. I call bullshit. Your past is what makes you. I don't think it's good to ever forget that. But pulling her picture out did a number on me, and I suppose the rest of the day I *did* slow down, maybe even regressed, because I taped it onto one of the bookshelves, put a record on and laid in bed, grabbing another nap before the stakeout.

***

I woke to the chime above the office door, and before I got a chance to get out of bed, I heard it again. When I went out to the desk, no one was there, just a folded note on the counter. It was from the young girl in apartment #2. She signed it *Shannon.* I knew it was her because the note said: *"Thank you for the $. Sorry."*

I got back on the computer, launched the browser, typed in Audrey's name, and hit search before giving myself any time to think. I didn't really know what I was looking for, but after clicking a few links, then adding "Los Angeles" to my search, an address and phone number popped up with the option to pay a premium fee for even more information. I already had everything I needed. With my gut full of barbed wire, I wrote the address down on a piece of paper, folded it, and stuck it in my pocket, then stood at the office door watching traffic, while my heart rate slowed to normal and the nausea subsided.

Chapter 10: Get in the Van

Roddy and I planned to meet in the parking lot at 10:00 p.m. In the meantime, I picked up trash around The Owl, keeping my eye on the hedges in case our guy made an early deposit, though I didn't invest much in that. The human body has a fairly strict schedule when it comes to moving the bowels. Then again, if you've got the squirts like this guy did the night before, anything goes.

I was sitting in Coltrane by 9:45, listening to some Ellington, my eye on the hedges. I'd brought the notepad, some sandwiches, a six-pack, and a bag of kale chips from the cupboard. Stale or fresh, I couldn't tell. It was my first foray into the world of healthy junk food.

Just before 10:00, I saw Roddy's door open and two legs emerge. Sort of. Roddy had on his same one cut-off, but instead of a stump poking through the denim fringe, there was a prosthetic leg clearly shorter than his real one, causing one hell of a limp.

He climbed into the van, didn't even look at me, and said, "You were right. Besides, I'm too old to be hopping around. It's hell on my back."

"Okay...but you may want to get yourself one that fits."

"Shit, you can tell?"

"A little bit."

"She's old. First and only prosthesis I've ever had. Hit a growth spurt at 20. But I figure should we need to set chase then I'm better off with than without." He set a backpack down behind the seats, then slapped his real knee. "You ready?"

I started the van, pulled onto Sunset, then drove half a block away and parked with the windshield facing the courtyard of The Owl. A perfect view. If anyone so much as farted near the bushes, we'd see it.

Roddy looked at his watch. "What time is bedtime for you?"

"Been sporadic since I moved, but I took a few naps. I can take first shift."

Roddy looked at his watch again, fiddled with it. "I'm usually out by midnight. We'll hang out, maybe I'll sip on one of those beers with ya."

"I brought food."

"We'll do that too. Afterward, I'll zonk out and you wake me at 3:00. Sound all right?"

"Perfect."

We saw Crystal-Anne walk out of Paradise Island, and Roddy made a remark on how it sure didn't look like she'd had two kids. I agreed.

For the next two hours, while sharing the kale chips and sipping on a few beers, Roddy and I got to know one another a lot better. I even told him about Audrey and how I still loved her.

"When you're at a crossroads like that, you don't have time to think. You stop to think, and what you assume is logic will rob you of your dreams. Love isn't logical. Not in our understanding of it. And if it were, it'd be boring as hell and never worth chasing."

I let the words sink in as we sat in silence, looking down Sunset at the lights. They have a way of lifting your spirits, and I wondered if the homeless camped in L.A. for the weather, or because the city can't help but make you feel like you're never alone.

The alarm on Roddy's watch went off with little beeps. He hit a button on the side, silencing it.

"That's my cue, Amigo. I've got her set for 3:00. Wake me if you see ass on grass."

Roddy made his way to the back of the van, took off his leg and set it on the floor, then got in the bed. Five minutes later, he was snoring.

***

Within the first hour, the only event involving feces I noted was Crystal-Anne letting a small dog out to do its business. Dogs weren't allowed at The Owl. Neither were cats. But I'd gotten no complaints of barking, hadn't heard it myself, and I'll be damned if I was gonna take away the only thing those kids had to keep them company while their mama was off showing her tits.

Anne was in pajamas. They were modest, hid all her woman bits generously. You'd never know there was a stripper under there. She was in mom mode, which I think probably reflected the real her more than a tight blouse and skirt. The poor woman lived two different lives, and I thought on how it must take effort to wear a smile at work.

The dog did its thing, and Anne took the time to pick up the mess, put it in a plastic bag, and toss it in the dumpster. That old dumpster had seen a lot of turd lately.

Soon after Anne went back inside, Wayne showed up. He was carrying a paper bag that no doubt held whatever alcohol he managed to acquire. I watched as he searched the grounds like a dog sniffing out a spot to lift its leg. Then I realized he was on the hunt for cigarette butts, something he could pull a few hits from. He finally spotted one worthy and picked it up, lit it, took a few drags and blew the stale smoke toward the sky. Then he took a sip from the paper bag and flicked the butt across the parking lot.

I was ready to wake Roddy, let him know shit was goin' down, but I waited to make sure, so I just watched Wayne through the binoculars. He was the snake in the grass, and I was the eagle, waiting for the moment where I'd swoop down and catch him in the act. But Wayne never dropped trou. He just bent down between the bushes and spread out a small blanket he must have had hidden, then laid down and hugged himself.

I felt it safe to rule out Wayne. That was his bed, not his toilet. I still kept watch but figured with Wayne tucked in, the guilty party wouldn't show. Or choose another spot to desecrate.

I set the binoculars on the dash and pulled the address I'd gotten for Audrey out of my pocket. I memorized it, whispering the thing over and over again. Part of me wanted to forget about the stakeout, wake Roddy and ask him how to get to Brier Avenue, do a whole other kind of stakeout. Stalking an ex isn't in my character, but sitting in the van, in the dark quiet, there wasn't much else to think about other than how much I missed that woman, wondering if she was alone and missed me too. But as it crept closer to 3:00 a.m., with no sign of the shitter, climbing in the back and getting to bed was the only thing I had the energy for. And before I knew it, the quiet beep of Roddy's alarm had me doing just that.

***

Roddy woke me two hours later. There was urgency in his voice, and I scrambled to the driver's seat with an impressive amount of speed and agility considering I'd been deep in the arms of sleep, dreaming of Audrey and how we'd bought a house on Brier Avenue, wherever that was. We owned a dog and two cats and decorated the trunk of a giant palm tree out front with Christmas lights every December. She was a real estate agent and I built muscle cars from the 70s. I don't know the first thing about cars.

"We got our guy!" Roddy nearly squealed, then handed me the binoculars.

I looked through them, and sure enough, there he was, pants around his ankles and squatting in the same spot he'd slept all night.

Bush-Guy Wayne was shitting in his own bed. I didn't see that coming.

"Okay, now what?" I asked.

"Gun it!"

I started the van, threw it into gear and floored it onto Sunset. My high beams ran across Wayne, whose eyes went dinner-plate wide. In a manner of seconds, we were pulled into The Owl, spotlighting him. He still hadn't moved, his bare ass hovering over the ground, arms wrapped around his gut. I could tell he was still suffering from the squirts, not even trying to hide the fact he'd been caught. I felt a little bad for him. I know what it's like to be at the mercy of your bowels. There've been moments where not even a house fire could've torn me away from the porcelain. Wayne wore that same face, clutching his belly and prayin' for mercy.

It was an uncomfortable moment for all of us. Roddy and I stood there waiting quietly, offering as much privacy as we could under the circumstances. Then Wayne made a run for it, right after he reached around, grabbed a handful of stool, and threw it. Just like a damn monkey.

The shit sailed between Roddy and me, and hit poor Coltrane square on the hood, landing with a dull thud and flattening into a patty the worst kind of brown-green you've ever seen.

Wayne's run was hindered by his fallen pants, which made the getaway more of a dance than anything. He didn't get eight steps before falling and shredding his knees on the parking-lot pavement.

Then he said, "I'm being poisoned!"

My first thought was of course he is. The guy's probably eating out of four different dumpsters on the daily, so I said as much.

"I don't eat garbage." He scrunched his face and grabbed his belly.

"Yeah, you don't shit in the bushes either," Roddy said.

"I got good reason for that."

Roddy looked at me. "I gotta hear this."

"Can we get you to pull your pants up first?"

Wayne let go of his stomach long enough to fetch some napkins from his pocket and wipe his ass a few times, as well as his pitching hand.

"We was at the park...aww shit this hurts...he left his bottle on the bench. He knew I'd drink it...and I did. But he spiked it with something." He paused, gave a pained looked and squeezed his stomach with both hands. "...and I don't think that's the first time he got me. I'm tellin' you...he's trying to kill me."

I gave him a moment to get his pants up.

"Well, I don't know anything about Charlie's beef with you, but—"

"That's what I'm getting at. I know I've been caught red-handed..." There was a joke in there about being brown-handed, but I saved it for later, when Roddy and I were celebrating the case being solved. "...but he has it out for me. The asshole started showing up about a month ago, trying to move in on my place. I'd come back here dead tired, ready for bed, and he'd be curled up, fast asleep right there in my spot."

"So, you started shittin' in your own bed so he wouldn't sleep there."

"I had to, man. I tried being nice about it, but he wasn't having it." Wayne paused again, gripped his stomach. "He declared war. The guy really had it in for me, had it in for Luna, too. Used to watch her through the window."

"That sonofabitch!" Roddy blurted.

"Why wouldn't he like Luna?" I asked.

"Evan said it was cuz he was buggin' people. He'd beg for money in the parking lot."

"Just like you."

63

"Yeah, I guess so."

"And now Evan's dead, too." Roddy said.

"Evan was a clumsy prick, that's all." Wayne scrunched his face. "Charlie didn't do that."

"What about tea-time Tuesdays?" I asked. Both of them looked at me like I'd just sprouted bunny ears and danced the Carleton. "Didn't she give him tea on Tuesdays?"

"Tea on Tue—? I don't know anything about that, but I believe Evan. That Luna ran Charlie off...and I think that's why he killed her."

Chapter 11: Lights Out

It didn't feel right investing in anyone who flings their dung around, but all this talk of poison, peeking in windows, and the idea someone as healthy as Aunt Ruth would just die in her sleep, didn't sit well with me. I had no choice but to inquire further about Wayne's accusation.

"Okay, hold on. Kill her?"

"Yep, broke right in and poisoned her."

"Broke in? You saw him?"

"Not exactly, but you do the math." Wayne tried to stand, and his knees buckled. He sat back down, putting a hand to his forehead—his clean hand.

"I can almost understand you protecting your bed with a pile of shit. Almost," Roddy said. "But somebody breaking in and poisoning a sweet soul like Luna? I'm not buying it."

I thought of Charlie and how he knew where everything was inside Aunt Ruth's: the ginger, the silverware drawer, the straws.

"I don't feel so well, guys."

That was the last thing Wayne said before he fell over, knocking his head on the pavement.

I checked his pulse. It was there, but he was out cold and limp as a ragdoll. I called 911. The case of the mystery shitter had been solved, but what we faced now was on a whole other level. An actual murder mystery. Or maybe just the overactive imagination of a crazy drunk with a penchant for marking his territory the likes of an animal.

***

The paramedics asked if Wayne had taken any drugs. I told them I didn't know but that he claimed he was poisoned. When they saw his shit-smeared hand, they wrapped it in a towel like he was a leper. By the time they left, Wayne was still breathing but not conscious. He didn't look good either, and I wasn't sure we'd ever see him again.

Roddy and I had a talk about whether or not we should take Wayne seriously. I shared with him my encounter with Charlie and why I thought the poisoning accusation could have some merit to it.

"Hell, I'm not sure what to think," Roddy said. "You see these fools passed out any time of the day. Crashed out in a bed of piss, empty bottle cradled in their arms, or a needle pokin' out of 'em. Wayne could have more habits than just a bottle and shittin' the bed. But if Luna was harmed...she deserves justice."

"Is it that easy to get away with killing someone?"

"If Wayne's right, apparently so."

The thought was unsettling, and that case-solving excitement didn't stir, but instead there was a righteous anger, one I could sense in Roddy, too. Maybe even more so.

"Some gossip from an asshole who accidentally hung himself, and accusations from a guy who shits his own bed, *on purpose*...We're nuts for lending a single thought to any of this. But if there's some truth to it, we can't just let it go, Jinx." Roddy's eyes were fixed on mine. He was ready with or without me.

Chapter 12: Crossroads

We knew we couldn't just track Charlie down and rough him up. The vengeful seed Wayne planted entertained the idea, but neither one of us was ready to trust his word as gospel. And neither Wayne nor Charlie gave us any reason to believe one way or the other. One of them slept in shit, the other one wore it.

After cleaning up Coltrane and spraying down the lot, Roddy and I hit a local diner and talked over bacon and eggs, neglecting sleep until later.

"I don't suppose you're friendly with local law enforcement, maybe have some pull to have my aunt exhumed?"

"Woah. That's jumpin' in way too deep and way too early, my friend." Roddy said. "You'd need a hell of a lot more to go on than what we've got."

"Probably. But if Wayne dies?"

"Still not sure they'd listen. The law don't like being wrong. They're prideful pricks. You have Luna's death certificate and all that?"

"Lawyer sent it in the mail. Haven't gotten it yet."

Roddy wiped his chin stubble free of bacon grease. "He sent it here? Or to your old address, in Washington?"

"Shit!"

"May want to give him a call." He took a bite of eggs, shoved in some bacon.

"I will. You don't suppose if we show up at the hospital they'll give me some info on Wayne."

"Hell, no. Not with that HIPAA shit." He sounded out the acronym like it was a word.

"You know Wayne better than I do. We chasing our tails here?"

"I may have seen him around more, but I know as much as you. He's homeless, a drunk, and apparently no corn in his diet."

I set my fork down and waved for the check, appetite ruined.

"Sorry."

"It's fine. I need to get to bed."

Roddy hurried the rest of his food into his face and washed it down with OJ, then wiped his hands on a napkin and said, "So, we're at a crossroads. We either entertain the idea Luna was murdered and the guy's running free. Or we head back to The Owl and play our every-day roles of one-legged handyman and love-lost property owner."

"You paint such a bright picture."

"Just sayin'."

"I don't know that I can ignore it, Roddy. There's women and children living in that building, and if someone's out creepin' around windows, well..."

The waitress slapped the ticket in front of me and asked if that'd be all.

"I don't suppose there's a phone number on that, too." Roddy gave a ridiculous grin he'd be embarrassed of had he seen it himself.

The waitress put on a half-assed smile, one of many in her arsenal used to maintain a tip, then walked away.

Roddy looked at me. "Can't help it. You any idea how long it's been?"

"At least stick to your league."

We both looked at the waitress, young enough to be Roddy's granddaughter.

"Aww, hell. A man can dream," Roddy said. "I got the bill, you tip."

"You sure?"

"I'm on social security and disability, and I get paid under the table to clean up shit and change locks. I'm sure. I've got more money than you might think for an old man who lives in a dump like The Owl...no offense."

I pulled a five from my wallet and set it on the table. "So, this crossroads, which way you leaning, handyman?"

"First thing's first. We need some sleep."

"Head home, catch a nap, then head to the hospital? Have another chat with Wayne?"

"Yep...if he's still breathin'."

**

I put on a record, jumped in bed fully clothed and wondered if I shouldn't hire some part-time help to work the desk. The way I understood it, a place like The Owl needs someone around during regular business hours, and this was an area I was already failing in. The little bit of studying I did of Aunt Ruth's financial records made it seem like hiring help was economically feasible.

She had no mortgage payment, only annual taxes, and Roddy had done a fine job at upkeep. No impending problems with electric, plumbing, mold or critters. The Owl was in great shape.

I finally fell asleep knowing exactly who I'd hire. Just so long as she accepted the offer, which might prove difficult if our first interaction was any indication.

Chapter 13: Nipping the Bud

I managed to get some sleep in before a knock at the office door woke me up.

I dragged myself out of bed and peeked around the corner. It was the stoner I'd spooked yesterday. The one in apartment #7. By the look of his slit eyes, I could go back to bed for another hour and he'd still be entertained by the wood-grain design on the door, because it sure as hell kept his attention now.

I stood and watched him for a minute longer, waiting for another knock. But he just stood there, zoned out, like he'd forgotten what he was doing there in the first place. Finally, I answered the door and invited him in.

"Heyyy, you're the dude from this morning," he said.

"Yesterday."

He looked to the ceiling, like the answer was up there as to why he couldn't remember one day from the next. I saw a stack of bills in his hand and asked if he was here to pay rent. He came back to earth.

"Uh...yeah. That's why I'm here...to pay rent."

The part of his brain that should have told him to fork over the money was still at the back of the bus, in a window seat, taking in the sights.

"Okay, I'll take it."

"Oh, yeah...wait. You're the new guy? Luna's brother or whatever?"

"Her nephew. Name's Jinx."

"Right on."

I walked behind the desk and grabbed the rent book, gave him some time to catch up.

"Can I get a receipt, dude? You know...just in case?"

"Sure thing. Number seven, right?"

"Correct."

"And what's your name?"

"The Jeff."

"*The*...Jeff?"

"Correct."

I did a quick scan of the book, and sure enough Aunt Ruth had him signed in as "*The* Jeff."

He finally parted with his money and I stuck it in an envelope, set it next to the safe. I made a note in the book and handed him the receipt.

"Say, The Jeff...you're not partaking in any illegal trade out of your apartment, are you?"

He gave a blank stare.

"Are you dealing weed?"

"Am I dealing weed? Out of my apartment? Am I dealing weed out of my apartment?"

His response was all I needed.

"No. No, sir...wait. Are you looking for some?"

"No...The Jeff, I'm not. But I know the cops are keeping a close eye on the place after what happened yesterday."

The Jeff's eyes grew from thin slits to bright, blue marbles.

"Writing license plate numbers down, looking for heavy traffic and suspicious characters. I guess they really want to nip this in the bud, make an example out of the weed dealers."

"Yeah?"

"That's what I hear. I just wanted to make sure everything was kosher at your place. I'd hate to see you go to prison."

"Right, right. Listen, dude. I've gotta bail. I just wanted to say what's up."

"And pay the rent?"

"Correct. You have a decent day now."

The Jeff couldn't get out the door fast enough. I had a feeling he'd be cleaning up his apartment within the hour.

***

I sat at the desk for a bit, looking over the books. I put the money in the safe and made a phone call to Aunt Ruth's lawyer to have him send copies of everything I needed, but this time to The Owl. I was especially worried about not having access to the bank account. I didn't like keeping all that cash around, especially when it seemed Charlie knew where everything was, and, according to Wayne, had already broken in once before.

The lawyer said I could drop by the office and get the paperwork to avoid the wait. I had plenty of time to hit his office, then the bank, before seeing if Roddy was ready to head to the hospital.

But first I needed some part-time help.

***

I knocked on Shannon's door. She answered even quicker than last time and looked dressed for work—tiny, white shorts, a tank with no bra. It was sad.

"I want you to work for me." I said.

"I don't use a pimp." She started shutting the door in my face, again. I stuck my foot in the way.

"That's not what I mean. I just need help at the desk. Someone to look after things when I'm not around."

She looked down at my foot and gave me some serious stink-eye, so I moved it.

"Luna didn't need any help. Why do you?"

"I imagine she was around most the time, but I won't be."

"So, you want me to babysit the office?"

"No, I want you to work as my employee, doing employee stuff."

"Like?"

"Like answering the phone if it rings, be there if a tenant needs something, like to pay the rent."

"You trust me to collect rent?"

"You look too healthy to be strung out, so I'm not worried about you stealing from me."

"Why else would I be trickin'?"

"Because you found an easy way to make a little money and don't have the self-worth to say no, despite how much you hate it. I think you think you're not better than that, but you are."

And like last time, I struck a nerve. She didn't know how to handle someone giving a shit. So, she tried slamming the door in my face again, and again I threw my foot in the way.

"You can start today."

"Do you have any idea how much I can make in one day?"

"As pretty as you are, and as sick as this town is, I would imagine quite a lot. And I'm sure whatever it is, I won't be able to match it. But what I'm offering will give you some self-respect and help you sleep at night. That's gotta be worth more than whatever it is you make."

She looked at me, studied me, making sure I was trustworthy. I didn't blame her. I can't imagine she held a very good impression of men, and I was hoping to be the one that showed her we don't all walk around with our dick in our hand.

"Today?"

"Right now, matter of fact. I'm still learning the place myself, but I can show you what I do know."

I could see her face trying to give birth to a smile.

"Okay, let me get changed."

"I do have one condition."

"What?" she sighed.

"You can't work for me *and* turn tricks. It's one or the other."

"How the hell am I gonna pay rent and buy groceries?"

"Well, I already cut your rent in half. Doesn't look like you've got a car payment or gas to worry about, so I think you'll make it. It might not be full time, but I'll make sure you work enough to have your needs met, and a little extra." I gave her about two seconds to think about it. "Meet me in ten?"

"Okay." The hint of a smile came back, and she shut the door.

***

I quickly made sandwiches in case Shannon hadn't eaten. She showed up in jeans and a T-shirt, her hair up and ready to work. I went over a few things with her, gave her my cell number and told her to call if she had any questions.

I asked her about Wayne and Charlie. She knew exactly who I was talking about and said she'd seen them both creeping about. Then I asked if she'd ever seen Charlie peeking through windows, or even climbing through any.

"No. Why? Is that something he does?"

"I'm not sure. Just make sure and keep your place locked up. Matter of fact, I'll have Roddy take a look at your windows tonight and make sure they're secure."

"Please do. I don't want any pervert climbing in my apartment. Kinda wish you hadn't told me that."

I didn't tell her about Wayne's murder accusation.

"Sorry. Just stay away from him."

Shannon hugged herself, like my words had been a chilly breeze.

"Should I be worried? Do you have a gun in here?"

"A gun? Uhh...no. No gun."

"What if he comes here while I'm working?"

I thought of tea-time Tuesdays. I'd make sure she wasn't working that day. If we didn't see him before then, it may be the only chance we'd have of finding him. And if we did, then what? A citizen's arrest? I thought about what Roddy said about the police being prideful, not liking to be wrong. Wayne's testimony was our only chance at the police taking a closer look at Luna's death.

"Peeking in windows doesn't constitute a bullet to the head," I said.

"Yeah. You're right."

"I'm sure you're in no danger." It felt like a half truth.

"Ummm...we didn't talk about pay," she said.

"You're right. How much is minimum wage around here?"

"I don't know."

"All right. I'll find out and tack on an extra buck. Sound good?"

She nodded.

"Later on, we'll get you some W2's, make it legitimate."

She gave me a blank stare. It was a question all on its own.

"Tax forms, make your employment legal. Pay some taxes, get some taxes. You got groceries?"

"Yeah."

"Okay, good. Seeing how you're all caught up on rent and don't seem to have other bills...do you?"

"No."

"No cigarette habit?"

"No."

"Okay, you're good then. I'll pay you next week, then every week after. It'll help you budget, force you to plan ahead."

"You sound like a dad."

"I do, don't I?"

"Yeah."

"I'll try and keep a leash on that."

I set a few dollars on the desk for the vending machine out front and told her I'd be back in two or three hours, then locked up my apartment and left for Roddy's.

Chapter 14: About Dyane

Roddy was up, making eggs and toast. Toast with ranch dressing on it. He saw me through the screen door and waved me in.

"You *do* love eggs," I said.

"At least twice a day. Want some?"

"Thanks, just ate a sandwich."

"What kind?"

"PB & J."

"With them kale chips?"

"Yeah." It sounded more like a sigh.

"You ain't hit the grocery store yet, have you?"

"I grabbed a few things."

"Apparently not enough if you're still eatin' that shit. Speakin' of things you need to do, you get a hold of that lost love of yours?"

"Audrey? Nah. Too busy with you, sticking our noses in other people's business."

"Hey, I'd call shittin' in our yard and killin' your aunt our business."

"You're not wrong."

"Have a seat. It'll be a minute."

I sat down in a padded metal chair covered in flowered vinyl, something that should have been tossed out 40 years ago. Other than the owl painting, the only other décor Roddy had was a photo of a pretty gal with feathered hair. She was standing on a rocky ledge overlooking beautiful countryside. The orange hue told me it was taken some time in the 70s.

"Who's that?"

Roddy scraped the rest of the eggs onto a plate with the ranch toast and sat at the table with me. "That's Dyane." He took a bite of eggs.

"Sorry. I shouldn't pry. It's a beautiful picture."

"Colorado. Daniel's Park at sunset. We were just kids then, spent all day in the mountains and all night workin' up a sweat between the sheets. Never even slept that night. It was magic. That woman had a touch that'd make you tremble. She used to say we were like two puzzle pieces that'd jumped off the table and ran from the others, and when we found each other, we fit perfectly. That's how soul mates are. Nothing short of a miracle, finding each other in a world with so many others, and you only fit in one place."

"She had a way with words."

"Yes, she did."

"What happened?" The conversation was already headed there.

"Bundy." Roddy pushed his plate away and drank from a glass of milk, looking over the rim at me.

83

"Bundy?"

"Yep."

"Not sure what that means."

Roddy set his glass down and stared into it, like it held secrets—a cylindrical crystal ball of cloudy white.

"The serial killer."

"Ted Bundy?"

"That's the one."

"Ted Bundy killed Dyane?"

"They never told me for sure, but how many people were in Colorado in '75 strangling women, bashing their heads in and tearin' up their insides?"

"Shit, Roddy. I'm sorry."

"It was a long time ago."

"Doesn't matter. That's a hell of a scar."

Roddy nodded silently. "He fried for it."

"Yes, he did. Don't suppose that helped, though."

"Nope. What's done is done. It didn't bring her back."

We sat in silence, and I suddenly became aware of the clock ticking somewhere on a wall. It was gunshot loud in that silence. Roddy downed the rest of his milk, picked up his plate, and set it in the sink.

"I was there the day he got the chair. Hitchhiked all the way to Florida, thinking it'd help." Roddy looked at the picture on the wall and rubbed at the stubble around his neck. "I was there before daybreak, along with a whole circus of folks. Most of 'em young locals looking for an excuse to sit around, drink beer and mouth off. There were even vendors selling souvenirs, Jinx. None of it sat well with me. I'm not sure what I thought I'd get out of going there. I think I was picturing me out there alone, thinking of Dyane, watching the prison lights go dim, knowing the man who killed my girl was being killed himself...but it wasn't like that."

"I can't even imagine. All this with Luna, I'll bet it really hits home."

"It certainly fuels me."

I let the necessary quiet linger for a moment, then changed the subject. "You ready?"

"I'll get my leg."

Chapter 15: Starter Kit

On the way to the hospital, Roddy bugged me about Audrey again. I told him I found her address.

"Wanna do a quick drive-by?"

It was tempting.

"Not now. Thanks, though."

"Your stomach's burnin' now, huh? I know the feeling. Every mention of an ex you can't let go of and your stomach starts cookin' up gas." Roddy rolled his window down. "Just in case."

"You ever find love again?...after Dyane?"

"I did. Twice. One I let go of years ago. The other, she's still on my mind. But she moved on, got herself married. She's a schoolteacher somewhere in California, but not near here. Not close enough to stir up the farts thinkin' I'll run into her at the store. Thank the Lord."

I rolled my window down, too. Just in case.

As I drove, Roddy and I both had our eye out for any sign of Charlie. There were plenty of homeless folks roaming the streets, sitting on the ground outside storefronts and even camped out in lots, but none with a greasy moustache, Panama hat and a halo of flies.

Without knowing Charlie's routine or regular hangouts, we knew we may have to wait until Tuesday, assuming he'd show for tea. But again, then what? Suppose we had him cornered at the office and he does what any guilty man would when confronted by two civilians who had no real proof or authority. He'd deny it. It'd be like hunting with no means to cook the kill, or collecting vinyl when you've got no turntable. Roddy and I discussed all this on the way to the hospital.

"What about wearing a wire? Get him to confess," Roddy said.

"Hide a mini recorder in my pocket? Hope he spills it like some Bond villain?"

"You've got a phone don't ya?"

"This." I pulled a flip phone from my pocket.

"Good Lord, man. The hell is that? You're what, thirty-two, thirty-three?"

"Thirty-four."

"You're thirty-four years old and carrying around a relic like that? Does it even have a camera?"

"No. Does yours?"

"Shit, I don't have no phone, 'cept the touch-tone in my apartment."

"Calling the kettle black, aren't ya?"

"The hell am I gonna do with a cellphone? Check the weather? Look at porn? The weather's the same every day, and I live across the street from a nudie bar."

"Well, what do *I* need one for?"

Roddy was quiet a moment, either frustrated because I somehow should have known better, or because I'd made a point and he was stumped.

"See that plaza up ahead? Pull in there."

"I thought we were going to the hospital."

"Just pull in. You'll figure it out."

As I was pulling in, I scanned the giant road-side sign, catching a glimpse of as many words on display as I could: *massage*, *pizza*, and *tattoos*.

"Well, considering we both just ate, I'm guessing either you want to get matching tattoos to commemorate our shit-investigating journey or you're wanting a quick happy ending, during a really inconvenient time I might add."

"Park over there." Roddy pointed toward a small storefront squeezed in between the pizza place and the massage parlor. The windows were covered in posters advertising deals on cellphones.

"I don't need another phone, Roddy. I'm a minimalist."

"Oh, bullshit. A new phone won't take up any more room than that toy you got now. Only, with a new one, you can get rid of all them records of yours. Kick your minimalism up a notch."

"Okay, first of all, no way in hell am I going digital. Second of all…" I stopped to think of a second-of-all.

"Camera, recorder, GPS…it's a P.I.'s wet dream."

"A P.I.? Who said anything about being a P.I.?"

"Who you kiddin'? I've seen that excitement on your face when shit's goin' down. And what you told me about wantin' to be a detective. Well, here's your starter kit."

"I didn't bring money."

"I did. I'll front ya." Roddy opened the door, got out, and limped around the front of the van while I sat there, realizing I didn't have much say in the matter and Roddy was probably right.

Like a child dragging his feet while shopping with Mom, I entered the store with all the reservation in the world.

"How much is this gonna cost me?"

"I won't lie. They're not cheap, but we'll get you a plan, knock a few hundred off the bill."

"A few hundred?"

"Told ya, they ain't cheap. You'll just have to trust me on this. You'll find a dozen ways to use it."

"I don't want games. I don't need that kind of shit. I've seen people with their face buried in their phone, playing Tetris or whatever."

"Boy, you've been living under a rock, huh?"

"I'm just not worldly is all."

Roddy raised an eyebrow like I was full of shit. "Wanna talk about that U-Haul full of records you lugged through three states?"

"That's different. It's music."

"Sure, if you're collecting every genre available to man, but all I've heard you play is jazz. How much jazz does one guy need? Shit all sounds the same."

"I got a nice collection of old school punk in there."

Roddy flapped his lips and shooed me with his hand "Even worse."

We bought the phone, and Roddy got excited after seeing mine, so he bought one too. We grabbed a beverage from the pizza place next door, and Roddy joked about getting a massage before we checked on Wayne. I think he was only half kidding, like he was waiting on me to pull the trigger, give the go ahead. If I had, I suspect we'd have found ourselves face down on a table while an Oriental woman rubbed us down, then I'd end up in the van, waiting on him while he crossed the finish line.

With brand new phones we didn't have a clue how to use, we made our way to Olympia Medical Center.

Chapter 16: Second Base

Like everyone else on the planet, I hate hospitals. Nowhere else does the appearance of sterility stir the gut into an anxious frenzy. Throw in the scent of bleached linens and suddenly you're contemplating life and death and whether you wasted your time on earth chasing the trivial or lived life to the fullest. Either way, you'll find a reason why it's never a good day to die.

That day, the glowing white halls of Olympia shed a light on my own life and what I've done with it, what I'd like to do, and where I'm headed. That episode of reflection was the catalyst for two things: the whole private investigator thing? I decided to go full bore, dive headfirst. I'd still run The Owl at the request of my aunt, but my true dedication would lie in helping others, be it snapping photos of adulterers or catching a killer. It'd be my career on the side. The second thing was Audrey. I had to know if there was anything still there, anything worth chasing.

In the meantime, Roddy and I made our way to the front desk, where one lady sat in a chair, her fingers fumbling over a keyboard, and another behind, flipping through papers in a manilla folder. Both wore scrubs.

"Hello, ladies. We're looking for a gentleman named Wayne," Roddy said. That's when it occurred to me we didn't know Wayne's last name, and getting any info on him might prove difficult.

"Are you a relative?" the woman at the keyboard asked.

"No," I blurted out. This got me a stern look from Roddy.

"*He's* not," pointing a thumb at me. "I am. I'm his brother."

"And the last name?"

"Great question." Roddy missed half a beat, then said, "He's gay."

The nurse and I both raised an eyebrow.

"He got married recently to his man-friend, took his last name. And for the life of me I can't remember it. Hell, we were *just* at the wedding, too. Wayne wore a nice dress and everything. My buddy here caught the garter. If he ever gets his head out of his ass, he'll be the next to get married."

Roddy gave me a sly side-eye. I had to give it to him. What he lacked in limbs, he made up for in quick wit and creativity.

The nurse fiddled with the keyboard and scrolled with the mouse, periodically looking at Roddy, most likely searching for a tell.

"Real skinny, ice-blue eyes, gray hair all matted like something could be livin' in it."

"Sir, we don't list them by description."

"Someone poisoned him. Will that help?"

"No, I'm sorry, it will not. We do have a Wayne Gracin, born in 1974? There's no street address."

"Helen, you can't give that information out!" the other woman said. She whisper-yelled it.

"That's him, Gracin." Roddy said. It was a guess.

The woman with the folders whispered something to Keyboard Lady that sounded like, *"He's downstairs now,"* and I got the feeling right away we weren't supposed to hear it.

Keyboard Lady's face went long, her eyes wide. "Oh," she said, then looked at Roddy. "Sir, just take a seat and I'll get the doctor. It'll be just a minute. I'm so sorry."

We sat in the waiting area, looking at our phones. I may as well have been learning to knit by staring at an afghan. It was all Greek, as they say.

"I didn't much like how she said that," I told Roddy.

"Said what?"

"*'I'm so sorry.'*"

"You caught that, huh?"

"Didn't sound good."

"No, it didn't."

We kept at our phones and swapped numbers. I even learned to take a picture. Where it went, I had no idea. But it was in there somewhere.

A doctor dressed in a white coat, loud tie and somber face, approached Roddy and me, and we stood. His face was a telegraph of bad news.

"You are Mr. Gracin's brother?" the doctor asked Roddy.

"I am."

"I'm afraid I have some bad news. Your brother passed about an hour ago."

"Aww, hell. I knew we shoulda come earlier," Roddy said.

"I'm very sorry, sir."

"Any idea on what killed him?"

"It's too early to tell, but your brother had a very unhealthy liver. I think that may be a contributing factor."

"What about poison? He said something to us about someone poisoning him."

"The paramedics did mention that, but we won't know anything until the labs come back. To be quite honest, I'm a little surprised Mr. Gracin made it as long as he did, considering the condition of his liver."

"So, the cause of death, that's the medical examiner's job at this point, right?" I asked.

"Yes, it is."

"Okay. Thanks, Doc."

"Again, I'm sorry for your loss."

The doctor nodded his head and gave one last sympathetic look before heading down the hall.

"Well, I'm beginning to think the only poison Wayne ever had was too much Mad Dog," Roddy said.

"Sounds about right, but I'm not giving up. Care to head downstairs?"

"Downstairs?"

"If he *was* poisoned, there's a chance they could miss it, unless they're specifically looking for it. I thought it'd be best we put a bug in the examiner's ear.

"You know, they don't just let you walk in there," Roddy said.

"What if they do? What if it's that easy? Just a matter of acting like you belong."

"And if we get caught?"

"You seem to be pretty good at coming up with something on the fly. You got us this far."

"I suppose we could pretend we're lost."

"See? You're already on it," I told him.

"You're a troublemaker, you know that?"

"Says the guy jumping on alligators."

"Jackass."

After Roddy gave a wink at the nurse behind the desk, we headed down the hall to the elevators.

***

We took the elevator straight to the basement. While not as much care had been taken aesthetically as the first floor, the basement was no dingy, neglected haunt with flickering lights. The biggest difference was the floor—a light blue-green tile never upgraded with the times, the color adding to the already depressing nature. The hall was narrow, long, and empty, except for a single sheet-covered gurney holding a stack of silver trays like morbid leftovers in a deserted hotel.

After hitting a fork in the hallway, we turned left, prompted by the only light beaming out from one of the door windows. A peek in the window revealed our instincts were right. Inside was a well-lit room filled with all manner of shiny stainless steel and a portly man wearing headphones, standing over a table which held a naked female corpse.

Roddy watched the man through the tiny window while I thought on what to do next. "Okay. We'll head in and just flat out ask the guy to keep an eye out for poison. Maybe he'll help us out."

"Yeah, I don't think so. Get your camera out...*now*!"

I went for my phone and struggled to turn the damn thing on, let alone find the camera.

"This guy here is a whole other kind of freak. Got the camera goin'?"

"I'm tryin'."

"Put it on video. We're about to find out everything we need to."

"What's going on?" I stuck an eye up to the window, my head hitting Roddy's. The portly man had his hands on the pale-blue tits of the cadaver, kneading them like dough. I know about as much as the next person when it comes to autopsies, but I don't think the procedure consists of a breast exam the likes of this, particularly with no gloves on.

"You filming yet?"

"Give me a sec." I found what I believed to be the record button, pushed it, and saw the ticking of numbers as the video rolled. "Okay, got it."

"Keep filming. I'm gonna open the door. He's got headphones, probably won't hear us. Get as much of this as you can."

Roddy opened the door, and I held the phone out in front of me while the examiner continued with the kneading and the tweaking. He never so much as looked up to make sure he was alone. His next move was something of a kiss. All tongue. He bent over, licked the dead gal's lips, then parted them. I'd had enough.

"All right, asshole!"

The look on the guy's face was a million young teens caught jerking off by Mom. He stared at us a moment, probably hoping it was a dream, trying to figure out if a swing to his own neck with a nearby scalpel wasn't the best way out of this. I kept filming.

"This...this is a restricted area. Wh...what are you doing here?" The guy had turned a shade of pale that nearly matched his plaything on the table.

"Better question is, what are *you* doing here?" I asked.

"I'm a medical examiner. I'm performing an autopsy. Who the hell are you guys?"

"Well, before we walked in here, we were nobody. But now it seems we're the difference between a job and a wife..." I took note of the guy's wedding band. "...and some time behind bars."

"From performing an exam?"

"You weren't performing an exam, weasel dick," Roddy said. "You were clearing second."

"Here's what we're gonna do," I said. "You're gonna tell us everything we need to know about the cause of death of someone in here, but you're gonna be damn thorough about it. I've seen enough TV to know stuff gets overlooked. But with this particular guy you're gonna check every nook and cranny, specifically for poison. You're gonna pay even more attention to him than you were this poor gal here. You give us what we want, and we'll think about not showing anyone your necro porn."

"You're blackmailing me?"

"Listen, we're not asking for money. We're just asking for the truth. We need someone who's gonna put forth the effort, because the police sure as hell haven't."

"And if I don't find poison? You can't expect me to sway the cause of death. I'll be no accessory to murder."

"That's not what we're asking. We have reason to believe someone's getting away with murder by way of poison and it's going unnoticed. Now that you're aware of the suspicion, we were hoping it'd help bring the true cause of death to light. There's no funny business here."

"Not by us anyway," Roddy said, nodding at the corpse and raising an eyebrow at Portly Guy.

"We're just asking for a fine-tooth comb is all."

"This isn't a litmus test. This work is extensive and time consuming. You can't just look over my shoulder for a few minutes while a conclusion is made."

"That's fine. We know where to find you."

"So...you going to delete that now?"

"Hell, no."

"But we have a deal, right?"

"Leverage, man," Roddy said. "You'll see us in a day or two. In the meantime, keep your stiffy off the stiffs."

Roddy made an exit, and I followed, leaving Portly Guy sweatin' in his scrubs.

Chapter 17: Selfie

We stopped by the lawyer's office and got the paperwork, then back to The Owl to drop Roddy off and grab the cash I'd been hoarding in the safe. Shannon seemed to be doing okay, so I asked if she could stay another hour while I squared things away at the bank, said I'd pick up a pizza on the way back. She said that'd be fine.

It was closing in on rush hour, so there was a line at the bank. I fiddled with my phone some while waiting, and before too long found the video I'd taken. I turned the phone down and played it, then stood embarrassed, feeling old and out of touch, as I watched a two-minute video of my own face. I had captured nothing on that phone but my look of shock as I watched a man molest a corpse. We still had our leverage, though. Useless footage or not, we'd already scared our inside man into helping.

Feeling like a fool, I pocketed the phone. Seconds later, time stopped as I laid eyes on Audrey, who was standing in another line not twenty feet from me.

***

It wasn't necessarily my nerves that got me the hell out of there, but just how bad it looked. Downright stalker-like. I hadn't seen the woman in four years, and I show up at her bank in another state? No. The time would come, but not like that.

As I ran to Coltrane, my stomach jumped in my throat and my balls shot north like they'd been dipped in ice water. With sweaty hands on the wheel, I headed back to The Owl, forgetting the pizza. Once I saw Shannon, I made like I preferred delivery and that she hadn't told me what she liked on hers. It was a lie, but I wasn't gonna try and explain to a 16-year-old that grown men still run from girls when they're older.

I'd lost my appetite but ordered anyway and forced a slice down while Shannon and I talked. She told me a little about her family—her half-brother in Santa Barbara being the only one she still kept in contact with. She told me about her dreams of being an artist and how she'd let go of that recently. Then she got tired of my pep talk about how she should still chase those dreams and went home. I don't know what's worse, being young and not realizing rough times pass, or being older and knowing your carefree days are behind you.

***

I tossed a record on and did some push-ups. I couldn't get Audrey out of my mind. She looked beautiful. Better than ever. Midnight silk hair, green eyes that'd twinkle even in the dullest light, the corners of her mouth forever threatening a smile. Everything I ever felt for her came rushing back in one giant wave of too much to handle.

When my appetite returned, I grabbed a few beers, the rest of the pizza, and headed over to Roddy's. He dipped the pizza in ranch dressing while we talked about what happened at the hospital, then he asked to see the video. Reluctantly, I showed him. He did exactly what I thought he would: laughed his ass off until he was rubbing tears away.

"You know, as long as I'm alive you'll never live that down, right?"

"I figured as much."

I told him about seeing Audrey at the bank.

"I say we go over there right now," he said. "Walk right up to her house and knock on the door."

"I can't do that to her. What if she's married?"

"Well, if you would've used that keen eye of yours and looked for a ring instead of shittin' yer pants, then you'd know."

"I'd like to think anybody would've done the same."

"Guess I heard of dumber things done for love." Roddy looked down at his missing leg, then back at me. "How about another stakeout?"

"Hell no!"

"She know your van?"

"No."

"Then there's no reason not to. That last stakeout was a good time. Made me feel young again."

"And risk getting caught spying on her? No way."

"Quit bein' a pussy. Let's just drive by. See how many cars are in the driveway, maybe catch a glimpse through the window."

"You gotta promise me that's all we're doing, driving by."

"You'll be the one behind the wheel."

"I just don't want to get there and hear more of your peer pressure bullshit."

"You're a grown man. You can make your own decisions. I'm just here to help." Roddy threw me a smile I didn't trust.

***

We drove down Brier Avenue—slowly—and found Audrey's house. There was a single car parked in the narrow drive. No cars out front. It was a small house, couldn't have been more than two bedrooms, if that. Something a single person might rent.

"The lawn needs cutting, and there's no flowers out front, no landscape," Roddy said.

"You that desperate for work?"

"I'm just saying there's no pride taken here. My guess is she's only renting. People don't waste time and money on a place they don't own. And I'm guessing if a man *were* around, he'd be taking care of the lawn either way." Roddy took a deep breath and sighed. "We're already parked, may as well mosey up and tell her you're in town."

I'd stopped the van and hadn't even noticed. "See? I knew you'd be pushing for that."

"Hey, it's not like you moved here to stalk her. You got yourself an inheritance. Hell, you were practically forced here. What happens if she sees you out in the wild like she almost did today? Now *there's* an awkward meeting."

"I'm just not ready. It's bad timing."

"What would you consider good timing?"

"Being settled in, I guess."

"You own a toothbrush and some records. What's to settle?"

"Shit's just weird at The Owl right now. You know that."

"If you don't do something quick, you may regret it. Keep that in mind."

"Will do."

I drove away hollow and confused. I think Roddy sensed that, as he took the time to point out landmarks, directing me on detours down streets that held beautiful landscapes and gorgeous homes. We had a laugh or two, swapped stories, then drove back home where the night hid The Owl's ugliness under a blanket of shadows and neon.

Chapter 18: Trouble in Paradise

The next day, I went shopping for groceries. This time, I bought too many. But the fewer trips the better. If I was ever going to run into Audrey again, it'd be at the store.

It turns out I didn't have the freezer space for everything, I had two loaves of bread and twelve pounds of chicken and beef that didn't make it. I set them on the counter to give to Roddy, and if he didn't have room then I'd go door to door until someone could use it.

I spent the rest of the day cleaning up the office, tossing stuff from the desk I didn't think I'd need. Aunt Ruth had a lot of paperweights and paperclips and way too many pens and pencils. By the time I was done, the desk was nearly bare, save for the rent book, the monitor, mouse and pad, and pencil holder I suspected Aunt Ruth made herself, as her initials were carved on the bottom. I put two pens and two pencils inside.

I made myself a tuna sandwich with onions and pickles and grabbed a bag of chips. Real chips. Then I opened a beer and headed out to sit in the back of Coltrane to watch traffic. Coltrane had become my porch. I didn't like being inside the apartment. I enjoyed the sun too much, and at night I enjoyed the lights.

I downed the sandwich and half a bag of chips, then sipped on the beer. Time flew by and the sky darkened a hazy purple-red. I saw Crystal-Anne leaving work, but this time she had her work clothes on, which was nothing more than a red bikini that shined like fire under the boulevard lights. She was holding a change of clothes in a messy bundle up to her chest, running barefoot across Sunset. I looked at my watch, expecting it to say 10:00. It was just after 9:00. When she got closer, I could tell she was upset.

"Hey, Anne. Everything alright?"

She made her way over.

"Are you stalking me, Mr. Jinx?" She tried to smile, but it was lazy and unconvincing.

"Just doing my thing, watching the world go by."

She sat next to me, and I scooted over.

"Maybe I'm too used to it, but I see no beauty in any of this." She waved her hand at the street and all its glorious, nighttime glow.

"You're avoiding the question. What's goin' on?"

"Nothing I can't handle."

"Something at work?"

I noticed her upper arms were discolored and welted, thick red lines where someone's fingers had been.

"You got another beer?" she asked.

"I'll go grab one, but first you gotta tell me who did this to you."

"A regular. This accountant who comes in a few times a week, blows hundreds, maybe thousands, on lap dances. Some of the girls get extra if they give extra. But I don't do that shit, and he didn't take kindly to being rejected."

"You tell your boss?"

"He tends to look the other way with the big spenders."

"This guy, he's inside right now?"

"Yeah."

"What's he look like?" It was at this point I knew I was gonna get into trouble.

"Bald, silk shirt, glasses too big for his face, fake tan."

"I'll go get your beer."

It took everything I had not to run across the street the second she gave me a description, but I figured it was best I count to ten, try and keep my cool. So, I went and fetched a beer for Anne and got myself another. By the time I got back to the van, that little exercise in self-control hadn't worked.

"Here you go." I popped open Anne's beer and handed it over. "Save my seat," I said, then ran across the street toward the strip club. I could hear Anne shout something I figured probably had to do with leaving well enough alone, which probably would have been a good idea. But the thought of this poor girl's kids sitting at home alone while their mom gets roughed up by some douchebag with a hard-on didn't sit well with me. So, I like to think I went and did what any man would do for someone who can't do it themselves.

Despite not having seen a set of tits in longer than I care to admit, the ones filling Paradise Island didn't distract me from my mission. I scanned the crowd for bald heads and found one, but he had no glasses and was about as tan as a maggot in a puddle of bleach. After spotting a girl leading another baldy by the hand through a pink curtain in the back, I headed that way.

I found myself in a short hallway with three different doorways, all covered with curtains. Sapphire blue. I opened one without hesitation and got an eyeful. This guy had hair, slicked back and wet. Fortunately, neither the dancer nor the lap caught sight of me. I closed the curtain and moved to the next. It was 50/50 from here.

I threw the next curtain open and could tell right away this was the guy. His tan head shined like a bulb under the neon lights, and the grip he had on the woman's hair told me she was going through much of what Anne had only minutes before. This woman wasn't having it either. Baldy saw me and got about one syllable out before I had him by the collar with his bare johnson poking me in the leg like we were jousting.

There was no need for a wordy exchange. The guy knew. It was just a matter of removing the scourge from the building.

Whether by instinct or because I didn't care much for his lance jabbing me, I buried a knee in his crotch before pulling him through the curtain and into the hall. The guy didn't put up a fight. He saved that for women, I guess.

We made our way through the club, one hand clutching the back of his silk shirt—which by now had about one button holding it together—and the other balled into a fist, looking for an excuse. As we passed what I assumed to be the bouncer, with his broad shoulders and a t-shirt he'd probably outgrown back in grade school, the big guy yelled, "What do you think you're doing?"

"Your job," I said.

I don't think he knew what to do with that.

Once outside, I shoved the guy to the cement walk, where he coddled his now-limp pecker and bruised balls. Anne was standing there in her ruby-red suit, the beer in her hand. She looked at me and smiled.

"If I see you around here again, you'd best be holding a bouquet of flowers and a Hallmark card with the most heartfelt apology that's ever been written for each one of those ladies in there," I told the guy.

He scrambled to his convertible with both hands on his junk and not a word out of him. I feel I lucked out with that little incident. Shit could have gone south real fast. It could have been me on the ground with a lot less teeth and a bruised ego, neither of which I wanted to spare.

"This is the part where you cover me with your jacket and walk me home," Anne said.

I looked down at my t-shirt. "Would if I could. How about the walk home...actually, let's give it a minute. I'd rather not let Baldy over there know we can be found right across the street."

I took her hand and led her toward the parking lot, where I figured we'd hang around the most badass car we could find, let on like it was ours. I picked a shiny, black Mustang and we lingered there while Baldy left the club.

"You're kinda my hero."

I chuckled. "Call it civil duty. If it wasn't me, it would have been somebody else."

We walked across the street and hung out in the back of Coltrane, doors open, beers in hand, and we talked about her job. I encouraged her to find work elsewhere. She said she'd been through worse, and I told her that should never be her go-to, that she deserves better.

Before she went home to her kids, she gave me a kiss on the cheek. It wasn't a peck. It was gentle and lengthy, and I suspect had I turned my head it would have been much more than that. But the only thing on my mind, after smelling Anne's makeup and perfume, was Audrey.

Chapter 19: Test Results

Another day went by before Roddy and I decided to visit the hospital again and check on Wayne's cause of death. I'd finally made a successful trip to the bank and had Shannon work a bit each day, mostly to give her something to do, help keep her out of trouble and stick to the deal we'd made.

I kept my distance from Anne. I liked her company, but I sensed she had other things in mind, and I wasn't looking for anything other than friends. Besides, I don't think I could ever be with a woman whose goods were on display. Call me old fashioned, but I like to know I'm the only one who's privy to that kind of blessing with the woman I'm with.

Before hitting the hospital, Roddy wanted to treat me to some authentic Mexican. Him being from Texas, I trusted him. We passed by two different Taco Bells on the way. It was like giving them the finger.

Roddy directed me to a place called La Perez Cocina. It was a real greasy joint with paint-chipped walls and dirty floors. I think his real reason for choosing the spot was the waitress. A real looker. Complexion smooth as shark's skin and eyes big as plums.

"I've been thinkin'." Roddy loaded his mouth with a spoonful of red rice, then chewed while I waited. "Let's say…" More chewing. "Let's say we get there and find out he was poisoned, then tell the police our suspicions. You really think that's enough for them to start sniffin' around Luna's death? Hell, we don't even have the first clue where to find Charlie or even which direction to point the dogs."

"I thought on that, about all of it, and I can't say what the police will do. But as far as finding Charlie, I'm banking on Tuesday. You didn't see the guy. He's got a wild eye for tea. He'll be back."

"Okay, but should the police not catch on, we're back to us dishing out justice. We find out for sure, you gonna bring the hammer down on Charlie? Eye for an eye?"

"You mean kill him?"

"Yeah."

"Hell no! I'm not going to prison over this."

"Okay, just making sure. You didn't strike me as one who'd off and kill somebody. But I suppose you could say the same for Bundy."

"That's not our job, and I don't have it in me. Do you?"

Roddy took a bite of his burrito and seemed to ponder the question. "If I knew I was dyin' I would."

"You mean self-defense?"

"No, I mean like if the doctors told me I had cancer or something and only had a short while. I think I could do it. If I knew for sure he killed Luna."

"We need to keep in mind we've got shit for evidence, 'cept Wayne's theory, some of which came from Evan."

"I know, I know. So, whatdya think?" Roddy pointed at my plate.

"You were right. It's good."

"They got another hot little senorita works here nights, too. We'll come back another time and I'll introduce you...since you're pussyfootin' around with the one that got away."

"That's not a discussion I have the belly for right now, Roddy."

"All right, all right. Let's go see the perv at Olympia."

***

There were personnel in the hospital basement when we got there, so we pretended to be lost and wandered back upstairs for a while, hung out in the gift shop.

The shop triggered a memory. Audrey had spent some time in the hospital to have a uterine cyst removed. The cyst turned out to be benign, but there were complications, so her stay was longer than expected. It was quite the roller coaster. I wouldn't leave the hospital without her, not for work, not even to go home and shower when I turned ripe. But I did make a trip to the gift shop and bought a stuffed bear holding a satin heart that said *Get Well Soon* written in pink, italic font. It was nothing special, but she loved that stupid thing. It meant the world to her. She broke down and cried when I gave it to her, tears born from exhaustion, just wanting to get the hell out of there and be at home in bed, eating popcorn and watching romantic comedies. I've sat through so many of those damn things I could write one myself. Anyway, the visit to the gift shop with Roddy brought all that back. If this was one of those movies, I'd buy another bear and show up on her doorstep, where she'd break down again and take me in her arms—single and still in love with yours truly.

"Try again?" Roddy asked.

"This time we own the place. None of this 'we're lost' bullshit. I feel like a little kid up to no good."

"Got it."

We headed back downstairs to an empty hallway and peeked through the same door we'd seen the peepshow two days before. Portly Guy was sitting in his chair, wolfing down what looked like a bowl of SpaghettiOs. We went in.

The guy looked up from his bowl, saw us and rolled his eyes.

"Now, what kind of greeting is that?" Roddy said.

"How do you guys keep getting in here?"

"Lucky for them…" Roddy nodded at the corpse cooler that lined one of the walls. "…it ain't too difficult."

The man sighed. "Let's get this over with." He stood, set his bowl of SpaghettiOs on a small table with wheels, and walked over to a desk in the corner of the room. "I won't bother you with the technicalities, but the bottom line is there was poison in his system. Thallium to be exact. And if I'm perfectly honest, had I not been searching for it, it could have been overlooked. However, because of the extensive damage to his liver, it's hard to determine if he died secondary to the thallium or his alcoholic lifestyle. If I had to guess, I'd say without medical intervention he would have died within the year, regardless. Now, the trace of thallium doesn't necessarily mean he was purposely poisoned. Mr. Gracin was homeless, right?"

"Yeah."

"Okay, well, thallium isn't easy to come by. It used to be a component in rat poison, but that's been banned for decades. My guess is the guy found his way into a dumpster near an apartment being renovated, someone tossed out some old rat poison that'd been stuck behind a fridge for the last thirty, forty years. Matter of fact, thallium doesn't even have to be ingested. He could have inhaled it or gotten it on his skin. But as far as murder, I think that's a stretch."

"But you're gonna report your findings," I said.

"Best I can do is what I've already done. My report lists all lab results, including the finding of thallium, and I've made the recommendation it was a contributing factor in his death." He said it all in one long sigh, like he was bored with us.

"Okay, now what are the chances of you pulling some strings to have a body exhumed?" Roddy asked.

Portly Guy laughed. "You're kidding, right? "Like I said, best I can do is point out the thallium. I've already told you I'm not convinced this wasn't just carelessness given the deceased's circumstances, but you guys can head to the police station and tell them your concerns, though I'm telling you right now, they're not going to dig that deep on account of some homeless guy and the insistence of you and your buddy...now, how about that phone?"

I grabbed my phone and played the video for him.

"That's it? That's what you had on me?" The guy kicked at a chair, like a kid in the cereal aisle after his mom says no.

"That, and the knowledge that you're one sad sack of shit," Roddy said.

"Get the hell out of here." He pointed toward the door.

We walked out like a couple of kids who'd just clocked a bully at school, toothy smiles for days.

Chapter 20: Tea-Time Comes Early

We got back to The Owl and I relieved Shannon of duty.

"Charlie was here," she said.

"Shit-stink Charlie?"

"Yep."

"Why didn't you call me?"

"I tried. You never picked up."

I'd left my phone in the van while we ate. I grabbed the phone, swiped the screen, wasn't even sure how to check for missed calls. I was just looking under the hood, fiddling with wires. "I hate this piece of shit."

"That's a nice phone. You just don't know what you're doing with it."

"What'd Charlie want? How long ago was he here?"

"He wanted tea and left about an hour ago."

It wasn't even Tuesday.

"Did you give him any?"

"No. I told him to leave. He creeps me out."

"Dammit!"

"Did you want him here?" she asked.

"No...I mean, sort of. But not while you were here alone."

"Why? You said I wasn't in any danger."

"I may have been wrong. The other guy I asked you about a few days ago, Wayne?"

"Yeah."

I had her sit down, then told her everything.

"So, Wayne said Charlie poisoned your aunt and now Wayne's dead?"

"That's right."

She was silent. No words, just a blank stare. Then the chime above the office door rang, and both of us swung our heads.

"Hey, Shannon. You ready?" A guy in his 20s with a beard and a pair of shades said it.

"Yeah, just a sec."

"You okay?" Beard Guy said.

"Who's this?" I asked. It sounded more intrusive than intended.

"This is Steven. Steven...Jinx. Jinx is my landlord."

I nodded at Steven. He nodded back. We already didn't like each other. I had my reasons, not sure what his were.

"Everything alright?" Steven asked.

"Yeah. I'm fine. Jinx was just filling me in on work stuff."

"You don't look fine. This guy messin' with you?" Steven looked at me. "You messin' with her?"

"If you mean by cutting her rent in half and offering her an honest job, yeah...I'm messin' with her."

Shannon ran over to Steven, put her hands on his chest, and told him to calm down, that everything was okay. "He's a good guy, Steven. He's looking out for me, just like you."

"Yeah? Well, he'd better be keepin' his hands to himself."

"I hope to God that's your big brother, Shannon, because if not, I'm about to—."

"You mind your business, grandpa."

Shit. I couldn't have been more than 12 years older than him.

"Steven, let's go!" She pushed him to the door, opened it, and out they went. Steven and I kept eyes locked.

The two got in his car and drove away.

My cell vibrated, scared the piss out of me. It was Roddy. He'd sent me a picture of himself sporting a toothy grin and flashing an arthritic peace sign. The message said: *"I think I'm figuring this thing out. I'll skool you on it later, Kubrick..."* The Kubrick remark no doubt poking fun at my phone-filming debacle.

I looked up from my phone and Crystal-Anne was standing at the door, a six-pack in her hand. I opened the door.

"I look pathetic standing here, don't I?" she said.

"Not really. You look like you finally got some alone time and didn't want to spend it cooped up in the same four walls. I'm guessing that beer is a consolation prize for letting my testosterone get the best of me the other night."

"You're good."

"Nah...easy guess."

"The kids are with their dad."

"Good to hear. Kids need their dad."

She wore a smile that was a flirtatious thing I didn't know what to do with. It taunted and teased and told me she was up for it, and if I kept ignoring the signs, her next move might be an aggressive one I'd neither be able to ignore, nor want to. A woman like her, a single man like me who hasn't felt a thigh in far too long. That's a recipe for combustion. But there's heartache buried in that lust. I had no intentions past the beer and the skirt, and no desire to play father to a couple kids who deserved better than The Owl. I jump in the sack with their mom just to shine my rocks and I'm no better than the asshole I escorted out of the club. I had to send out my own signals before the gentleman became weaker than the pig.

"Tell you what, Anne. You're just about the prettiest woman I've seen since I've been here, but I need friends. That's all. I don't want to confuse you or your kids with any kind of silver lining, because there isn't one. That may sound noble, but it's not. Truth is, I want nothing more than to share that brew with you and find out what's under them clothes, but that's all it'd ever be. A roll in the hay with an uncomfortable aftermath, and the last thing you need is another man using you."

As I waited for Anne's response, the silence between us was a stone thrown in a deep well. Anne looked at me, her smile having faded, and for a moment I thought I'd lost a potential friend.

"First of all, that's awfully presumptuous of you...to assume I wanted anything more than to share a few beers and some conversation. But…" The smile returned. "Nothing seems to get by you, and you're right. I was hoping to show you what's under these clothes, and if it's any consolation, I'm not looking for anything more than a roll in the hay myself. You've no idea how long it's been since I've met a decent guy." She looked toward Paradise Island. "Gentleman's club my ass."

I chuckled. "I'll keep it in mind."

"The offer will eventually expire, Jinx. Keep that in mind, too."

"And I just may regret it...now, how about we split these beers and watch the boulevard. You like jazz?"

"Not particularly. I'm too young for that, and so are you. Got any metal?"

"Close. I've got some crossover in the van."

"Crossover?"

I took the six-pack from her and led the way to Coltrane, where I had some old D.R.I and Accused cassettes in the glovebox.

"You'll see."

Chapter 21: A Stiff Sentencing

I slept alone. And knowing I didn't have to kept me up most the night. I had the kind of sleeplessness not even John Coltrane's *Kind of Blue* would calm.

I hit snooze on my alarm half a dozen times until Roddy came pounding on the door with a plateful of pancakes, bacon and eggs. I would have hit snooze at least a half dozen more if it weren't for him. He asked about Crystal-Anne, said he saw her over here.

"Sorry," I said. "No Penthouse forum letter to report. She's a looker, just not for me."

"Something wrong with you. Who looks the other way with a gal like that? You need to get with this Audrey girl or get off the pot. Dig in or move on."

Roddy was a horny fella, and I didn't think he'd understand too much about wanting more than a piece of ass, so I didn't try proselytizing the need for something deeper. Even I wasn't sure I understood it. One thing Roddy was right about was moving on with or without Audrey. It was killing me. That knot in my stomach seemed a permanent thing now, and the sonofabitch twisted my shit all to hell and back. In the meantime, I needed to keep my mind off it and focus on the case. There was still a murderer to catch. Maybe.

I told Roddy about Charlie showing up and about meeting Steven.

"You think it was her pimp?"

"More like boyfriend. He seemed awfully possessive, even for a pimp."

Then we heard sirens. The sirens that accompany a big city, you get used to them. They're like crickets in the country. You don't hear them unless you're thinking about it, or unless one is closer than it should be, like these.

Four police cars pulled into The Owl, sirens blaring, lights flashing, followed by two unmarked black SUVs which parked haphazardly on Hamilton. Within seconds, The Owl's parking lot was filled with suits, badges, and unholstered guns.

They were headed for apartment #7. The Jeff's place.

The irony struck me straight away that I'd warned The Jeff only days earlier the police might be onto him. I was joking, of course, but I was hoping if the kid *did* have weed in there he was able to get it out. I knew they'd give him more time than he'd ever deserve if they found it.

Roddy and I stood by and watched the cops, and even what looked like S.W.A.T., rush the door and shout their credentials.

"Jeffrey Watts! LAPD! Open the door and exit the apartment slowly with your hands above your head!"

They gave that kid about two seconds to comply before they broke the door in. My first thought was who's gonna pay for that? My second was Roddy would finally have something to do. My third was how the poor kid inside probably just shit his pants, which seemed to be a trend around here.

There were no obligatory shouting commands once the cops breached the tiny apartment. No pummeling. No gunfire. Just silence. Then two of the officers exited the room with hands across their mouths, pinching their nose. I knew what that meant.

Roddy and I crept toward the door to get a peek inside. We were stopped by an officer with sculpted red hair and more freckles than the sky has stars. "That's far enough. Move along now," he said.

"I own this place. This here's my maintenance guy."

"I'll be fixing that door you just busted," Roddy said.

"Alright, but you don't want to get any closer."

As if on cue, I caught a whiff of what I assumed to be the early stages of decomposition.

The smell was faint. The Jeff couldn't have been dead for more than a few days, but I suppose between the summer heat and Death filling a dead man's pants—its idea of a joke—it was enough to repulse even at that distance.

Roddy and I made it to the threshold of the door. The Jeff was half on his bed, his face kissing the carpet. He wore a pair of briefs that'd been tie-dyed, with the center of the design being his ass—a lavender bullseye now stained brown.

"Any idea what happened?" I asked a different cop standing near us who had a moustache straight off from Burt Reynold's face in his prime.

"Nothing you need to concern yourself with."

"I own this place, and if that kid in there has been murdered, then you need to fill me in."

Roddy gave me a proud poke in the ribs.

"Who said anything about murder?" the cop asked.

"This is the third person who's died here in the past month. Four if you count the poor bastard who got himself caught in the trees over there, so it's a healthy guess. If you guys did your job you'd know that already." Another poke to the ribs.

"We've no reason to believe this was murder. That kid was a druggie."

"He was a pothead, not a junkie."

"Were you aware of the business Mr. Watts was running out of your motel?"

"It's not a motel, and I had my suspicions. But you guys need to keep your eyes open for thallium poisoning."

"And how would you know anything about that?" The cop gave a real interested look.

Roddy elbowed me in the ribs again. This time it was to tell me to shut the hell up. Our means of info by way of blackmail wasn't something we could share.

"A resident told us," Roddy spoke up.

The officer pulled out a small pad of paper and a pen. "Okay, what's the resident's name and room number?"

"He's dead, but before he died, he told us he'd been poisoned."

"I see. And was this recent?"

"Thursday morning."

"Which room number?"

"He didn't have an apartment here. He slept in the bushes."

"He was homeless?"

I could already tell the cop had shut us out.

"We also have reason to believe my aunt died the same way."

"Was your aunt homeless, too?"

"She was a saint!" Roddy yelled. "And she owned this placed, helped everyone she could around here."

"Calm down there, old timer. Best bet is to head down to the station with your concern. Right now, we've gotta take care of your dealer friend. And next time you suspect drug activity on your property, give us a call. Company like that only invites trouble, and it sounds like you've got plenty already."

"You guys get a big ole' boner for a bag of weed but people turn up dead and y'all can't be bothered." Roddy pulled off his cap and spread his thin, wet hair across his scalp, then walked away. I followed.

"Useless," Roddy said. "And he called me old-timer. I look that old to you?"

"Hell no. Don't let that prick stir you."

"It's startin' to feel unsafe around here. Maybe it's time for some door-to-door warnings."

"My thoughts exactly."

Roddy and I watched the medical personnel and blue suits walk in and out of The Jeff's apartment like ants—carrying stuff in, carrying stuff out. A truck came and towed his car away, but I had a feeling it was empty.

"Something doesn't feel right," I told Roddy. "Charlie ain't the most charismatic type."

"He's no Jim Jones."

"So, how's he getting all these people to drink the Kool-Aid?"

"I'm questioning whether this is Charlie's doing at all. Maybe we should broaden our view on suspects."

An hour later, Roddy and I had knocked on each door, putting the fear in each of the residents, warning them about suspicious characters, particularly Charlie but not limited to. I told them not to drink anything they hadn't broke the seal on themselves, while Roddy made sure each window was locked and secure.

Crystal-Anne was the most concerned, and rightly so. She had the two kids. I told her on work nights I'd check on them whenever I could. I also told her I understood if she didn't want to clean The Jeff's apartment. She was relieved, as it spooked her pretty bad.

Roddy stayed at The Owl and put a new door on The Jeff's apartment while I headed down to the police station and filed a report. They listened, took a few notes, then talked about what they were and were not able to do. They told me to call if I actually saw anyone climbing in windows or spiking drinks. Essentially, it was a dead end.

Come early evening, I was restless. I spun a few records, tried to get my mind off death and poison and people shitting themselves, then found myself in Coltrane, on my way to Brier Avenue once again.

Chapter 22: Bleeding Out

It was 8:00 p.m., and I was letting the Duke Ellington tape play out. Audrey was home. I saw her pass by the bay window a few times. I knew I wasn't going to leave without speaking to her. Before she left Tacoma, she told me if I'm ever in L.A. to look her up. Both of us knew that would never happen, yet there I was.

The last time I'd seen her—not including the bank—there were a lot of tears, a number of hugs, and the last kiss that ever meant a thing to me. I filed it away and pulled it out often. Other than our first kiss, it was the most memorable. It was the one that kept me humble, kept me hurting, and brought me back to her doorstep.

I crossed the street and went up to her door, knocked on it. My knees grew weak. When I saw her face in the door's window, eyebrows raised in surprise, my stomach burned like I'd eaten hot coals. Audrey's wide eyes grew crow's feet as she smiled maybe bigger than I'd ever seen. Seeing that felt like the hard part was over.

The door swung open and she was all arms around me, squeezing tight.

"Jinx! What are you doing here?" The question was filled with bewilderment, not concern. The hot coal in my gut went out and was replaced with the same butterflies that came to visit during our first year together. Banging their wings inside, letting me know I was alive, letting me know I was in love. Nothing had changed with those batting wings. They were familiar, and I never wanted them to leave again.

With the hug, I let go first. I didn't want to show I would've stood there in her embrace until the sun fell and rose again.

"Look at you!" She held me at arm's length. "You look great!"

I told her she looked better than ever and L.A. must be treating her well. Then I saw how she was dressed. Those weren't work clothes. They weren't casual clothes. She was going out.

She asked again what I was doing in L.A. I told her about Aunt Ruth dying and leaving me The Owl.

"The Neon Owl? On Sunset?"

"Not something I'm proud of, but it's nice finally getting out of Washington. I…should have come sooner." It just came out and we both knew what I meant. And that's when the timing went from bad to worse.

A car pulled in the drive and a man got out. A handsome one, with thick, dark hair and a jaw I could have sliced an apple on. It was her date. Audrey and I looked at each other, and she gave me this sympathetic smile that couldn't have felt anymore awkward if I'd had something hanging from my nose.

"Shit, I'm sorry," I said. "I didn't know you were busy."

"No, it's okay. I'm glad you stopped by."

Blade-Jaw walked to the front step and Audrey introduced us.

"Mike, this is my friend, Jinx. Jinx, this is Mike."

Friend. Man, that shit killed.

We shook hands, and I forced a smile. It was ingenuine, and I'm sure Audrey caught it.

"Well, listen...Mike, it was nice meeting you. Audrey, it was great seeing you again."

"It really was, Jinx." She reached for a hug. "So sorry about your aunt."

I snuck a whiff of Audrey's hair and tried to store it, keep it as long as I could. But it was gone after the first step I took toward the street.

"Don't be a stranger!" Audrey shouted.

I just smiled, raised my hand in a half-assed wave and crawled back to Coltrane, wounded and full of regret. I stuffed a mix tape in the cassette player and drove around L.A., familiarizing myself before heading home while Black Flag preached to me through Coltrane's speakers about nervous breakdowns, jealousy, and rising above. It was everything I needed to hear. The wound wasn't just re-opened. I was bleeding out.

Chapter 23: The Process of Weeding Out

It was late when I got back to The Owl, and just in time to see a woman leaving Roddy's place. I caught him in my side mirror under the glow of the brake light, giving her a peck on the cheek and a grab of her ass—an ass that barely fit in the skirt that hugged it. She squealed playfully and hopped in the driver's side of a modest four-door. Roddy stood at his door watching her, one hand in his boxers and the other on the door frame, his wispy hair in disarray like cobwebs stuck to his head. That little bit of hair had been worked over.

I stayed in the van with my eye on the mirror while the woman left.

"I have an interview process!" he yelled after spotting me.

"A what?" I opened the van door.

"Stay there, I'm comin'." Roddy hopped across the parking lot, his bare foot slapping on the pavement, then got in the passenger side. "Full transparency, she's a hooker."

"I gathered."

"But I have an interview process. I don't just run out and grab the first piece of ass that catches my eye. I don't want no druggie or thief in my bed."

"So, you interview them first?"

"A dinner date. I ask questions, feel them out, find the reason behind their career choice. And if I don't smell bullshit, then it's on. That there was Jenny. She's what you'd call a regular, I guess. It ain't easy finding a woman who meets the criteria. So far I've found two."

"You're serious."

"Not all of us have strippers waving their tits at us, Jinx."

"Hey, I'm not here to judge. It just threw me is all. It's good you've set some...boundaries."

"A code I'll stick with until my pecker falls off."

"Which could happen sooner than you like if you're not careful. So, no druggies, no thieves. What else is left?"

"Jenny's trying to get through school. She's a good girl with her own criteria, which I happen to meet." Roddy said that last bit with his chest puffed out.

"Well, you must have a hell of a bullshit detector."

"I get a little help."

"Oh yeah?" Roddy seemed to contemplate elaborating, so I pushed him. "Told you, I'm not here to judge."

"Yeah, we'll see." He got out of the van. "Come on. I'll show you."

We headed inside Roddy's place. He told me to have a seat on the couch, then got a small, leather pouch from the nightstand next to his bed and tossed it on the coffee table in front of me.

"That's my bullshit detector."

He looked at me, waited for me to pick up the pouch and start asking questions. I did.

"This your bag of voodoo?"

Roddy didn't smile.

I opened up the pouch and dumped out a handful of polished rocks of varying shapes, sizes, and colors.

"Okay, I've got a chicken-or-the-egg question for you. You get this hippie shit from my aunt or she get it from you?"

"I got it from her."

"You really believe in this stuff?"

"I knew you'd laugh."

"I'm not laughing."

"You're rollin' your mind's eye, that's bad enough."

"I just never had a reason to subscribe to the power of a rock is all. You prove me wrong and I'll reconsider."

"That's just the problem. I don't really know what the hell I'm doing. I used to watch

Luna with hers, and well...she put the faith in me with those things."

"Don't take offense, Roddy, but could that have more to do with you having a thing for her?"

Roddy seemed to consider the suggestion. "Maybe."

"You mentioned they helped with weeding out truth from lies, could be you're just a good judge of character."

"Could be."

Roddy's head hung low, like a kid who'd just been told Santa isn't real. I changed the subject. I could tell it was more than just some new-age mumbo jumbo to him. It was part of Luna, someone he cared for and missed.

"I went to Audrey's tonight."

"Oh yeah?"

"Her date showed up, too."

"Oh, hell."

"Roddy, she was more beautiful than ever."

"How'd she take your visit?"

"Pleasantly surprised."

"Pleasantly's good. You get a kiss?"

"A hug."

"A hug is good. She move in or did you?"

"She did."

"Sounds like it went pretty well."

"Maybe. She told me not to be a stranger."

"Then don't be. Don't turn this into a game, Jinx. That one where pride gets in the way. That shit's what may have cost you the last four years to begin with."

"So, you think I should show up again?"

"If you don't, you'll regret it. You play your cards right, you'll be walking down the aisle with her in a year's time...knock on wood." Roddy reached over and struck his knuckles on his leg that rested against the couch.

"Is that even wood?"

Roddy studied the leg a moment. "Hmm...not sure. Close enough."

"So, tell me what you know about these stones."

"Well, Luna used them for different purposes, particularly their supposed healing properties. She gave me a little book about them. I read it, but I'm not sure I get it, though not for lack of trying. 'I want to believe', as the TV agent said."

"What are they supposed to do?"

"Most of 'em I've no clue. I do like this one though, kinda pretty." Roddy held up a purple stone that looked more like a crystal. "Luna told me the fact that I'm even attracted to it could help align my chakras if I carried it around." He used air quotes, and I could tell it embarrassed him to say it out loud. "But I do know all about this one." He reached down the front of his shirt and pulled out a necklace with a shiny, blue stone wrapped in copper wire. "This one's called kyanite. It's the real bullshit detector. Supposed to help me connect to the spiritual world and give me insight."

"Okay." The only word I had.

"I realize it's a hard pill to swallow, and maybe some of this is like you said, that I just miss Luna. But I can't help but think there's at least a little something to it. Why else would she believe in it?"

"That I can't say. I think sometimes people hold onto whatever they can just to get by, and I think sometimes there's truth behind some of it. Maybe some of it's psychosomatic, like a placebo."

Roddy rubbed the blue stone and tucked it back into his shirt.

"I think I met Shannon's boyfriend tonight, and he's a douchebag," Roddy said.

"Told ya."

Roddy rubbed his eyes, smoothed his hair. "Alright, get on outta here. I'm off to bed. Jenny wore me out."

"Real quick, I saw a park a few miles from here full of homeless folks, camped out in tents and what not. Feel like heading down there in the morning? Someone's bound to know Charlie. He might even be there."

"Count me in."

"I'll pack us a lunch," I said.

"Tuna and cheese, but use ranch instead of mayo."

"On second thought, let's B.Y.O.B."

"You gotta try it," Roddy said.

"I'll stick with PB and J sprinkled with Doritos."

"At least you're thinkin' outside the box."

"Got to if you're a P.I., right?"

"Let's get you through this case before you start throwing titles around, kid."

"That stings."

I said goodnight and headed to my place. I saw the light on at Crystal-Anne's and thought about her open invitation. Interrupting Audrey's date and seeing for myself how she'd moved on felt like a good enough excuse to stray. But I thought of those kids again. Another guy through a revolving door. Another bit of false hope.

I went home, spun some Mingus and drifted off.

Chapter 24: Revelation in the Park

Roddy showed up at 9:30 a.m., a sack lunch dangling from one hand, a six-pack from the other. He made us eggs and toast while I showered, then he bitched about not having ranch dressing and ate his food down with a scowl.

I stopped by Shannon's to see if she'd watch the office. She wasn't home.

Roddy and I left for the park. We brought our lunches, the beer, and the binoculars. Roddy had on a hat and sunglasses—a stereotypical costume for the conspicuous. All he needed was a newspaper to peek over. I asked him if he had one. He told me to eat shit.

We picked a bench in the middle of the park under a tree in the shade. The park had a healthy amount of homeless folks camped out in tents and makeshift lean-tos. It didn't feel like a park at all but a camping ground surrounded by the constipated flow of L.A. traffic.

There was a man camped near the bench. He laid in the grass surrounded by backpacks, with his head—which was wrapped in a towel with a broken drumstick poking out of it—resting on a rolled-up blanket. He was reading a small new testament Bible and had a pretty bad cough, spitting bits of lung every few minutes. After the guy stopped reading, we asked if he knew anyone named Charlie and gave him a description.

"I don't know anybody's name around here. I give 'em my own names. But it sounds like you might be talkin' about Dysentery Gary. He's a chatterbox, likes to talk about the past too much. It's depressing, so I tune him out when he's gabbin'. But yeah, that hat and that 'stache. It's gotta be him."

"Anyone around here die recently?"

The guy gave me a look like I'd asked if he could point me toward the nearest tree.

"Your friend serious?" he asked Roddy.

"Okay, more specifically, have you heard of anyone being poisoned, or getting sick and dying? Nothing drug or alcohol related."

"Nah, nothing like that. You guys cops?"

"No, we're not cops," I said.

"You're wannabes."

"Something like that."

"Watch my stuff real quick. I gotta whiz," he said.

The guy ran off to the other side of the park, whipped out, and pissed on someone's two-man tent. The side of the tent turned dark, then shook violently as the person inside struggled to get out. We could hear cussing and yelling while the pisser ran back toward us, an open-mouthed grin full of nothing but gums and three teeth that looked more like golf tees.

"Thanks, boys," the guy said, then sat down next to his stuff.

"The hell was that?" Roddy asked.

"That there was a declaration of war. That peckerhead stole my shoes. Don't worry. He won't be coming over here. He's chickenshit, waits until I'm bottle-deep to mess with me...oh, by the way, I spotted your guy over there." He pointed.

"Charlie?"

"Same stupid hat, moustache like caterpillar roadkill."

I snatched the binoculars and looked. There, on the other side of the park, sat Charlie, though the peculiar part was Shannon sitting next to him.

Chapter 25: A Leak to Fix

"I don't get it," Roddy said while he looked through the binoculars. "We told her what Charlie might be doin', and there she sits, right next to him."

"Maybe we're seeing vigilante justice, and this is her makin' a preemptive strike, taking things into her own hands."

"You know...we talked about charisma before and Charlie's lack of." Roddy scratched his chin like it helped him to think. "Well, you can't say the same for Shannon. Who's not gonna trust a sixteen-year-old girl?"

"I know you're not suggesting she poisoned Wayne, or killed my aunt."

"The other day, when you told her Wayne had been poisoned and that we were looking at Charlie for it, what'd she say?"

"Nothing. I think she was stunned, probably scared the hell out of her. Then Steven showed up and we dropped it."

"She didn't say anything to Douchebag about it?"

"Not in front of me, no." I said.

"In hindsight, what do you think about that?"

"Not much."

"She look scared to you now?" Roddy handed back the binoculars. I looked through them. She just sat there, talking to Charlie.

"I don't see Shannon killin' anybody, Roddy."

"You gonna make me bring up Bundy again? Handsome. Charismatic."

"She's just a kid. You're graspin' at straws, man."

"I hate to suggest it, but you've got a key to her apartment sittin' there in the office."

"Dammit, Roddy."

"You *are* the owner. And I'm the maintenance man. Maybe there's a leak or a broken window in there that needs fixin'."

"Shit!...yeah, maybe."

We gave our lunches and the six-pack to the homeless guy, and left for The Owl. Apparently, there was a leak to fix.

***

Shannon's apartment was well kept. It smelled of lemon Pledge and citrus. In the small bit of free space she had, there was a bookshelf that held mostly books on true crime and psychology.

While I sat on the bed, thumbing through a personal journal, Roddy rummaged through her dresser, filled with nothing but modest clothing. Nothing in the apartment pointed toward a night life filled with prostitution. This was like the bedroom of a well-read, well-behaved high-school girl.

The journal revealed nothing. Each page was filled with drawings done in various colored pens and markers, the pages spattered with bits of poetic prose or random words. None of which seemed to be of any importance to our investigation. The journal was nothing but a typical daydreaming, young girl's thoughts on life, parental distress, love, and loneliness.

Next to the nightstand was a trashcan filled with tissue, wrappers, and crumpled paper. Roddy overturned it and dug through each piece of trash.

"Here we go, Jinx. How's this for a straw?"

Roddy handed me a crumpled piece of notebook paper he'd flattened. The paper had a short list of names with a few opinionated words after each. The handwriting was different than that in the journal. These were no bubbly letters often associated with a girl's writing, but a rough, scribbly mess. A man's writing. All the names on the list were familiar, two of them now deceased:

Wayne - Drunk beggar

Jeff - Drug dealer
Charlie - Drunk peeping tom
"It's a kill list," Roddy said.

"I'm not convinced Shannon wrote it, but whoever did seems to be cleaning house."

"Right. So, I'm thinking we should scoot, before we're added to it."

Before we had a chance to leave, the door opened, and there stood Shannon and Steven.

Chapter 26: Bittersweet Tea

With the list still in my hands and the journal open on the bed, there was no pretending we were there to fix a leak. At first glance, Roddy and I looked like a couple of perverts, giggling at the private, teenage meanderings written in a diary.

"What the hell are you doing in my apartment?"

We were two deer in four angry headlights. Both of us at a loss for words. I think I'd rather get caught greasing my pole than be in the position I was in that moment.

"She asked you a question," Steven said through gritted teeth.

I decided to turn things around. *I* would ask the questions.

"What were you doing in the park with Charlie?"

"That's a good question." Steven looked at Shannon, his face in hers, hands balled into tight fists. "What *were* you doing in the park with Charlie?"

"I wasn't there with Charlie, babe. He just happened to be there. I...I told you, I went jogging. That's all."

"Alright." With nostrils flared, Steven slowly turned back to me. He didn't seem entirely convinced. "So, again, what are you doing in her apartment?"

"You know what we're doing here."

Shannon did what she could to save face, test the water and make sure we were on the same page before folding. Can't say I blame her. Hell, I still wasn't sure exactly what her role was here.

"Are you evicting me? Are you tossing my stuff out?"

"That's certainly one way of looking at it."

Then Roddy spit the catalyst that took everything to the next level.

"Why Luna?"

"Ssshhhiiit!" Steven said, then pulled a pistol out of his waistband and took turns pointing it at Roddy and me.

"Steven! What are you doing?" Shannon gripped his arm. "They're not part of this."

"They are now." He pulled away.

"Hold on there, son. You don't wanna do that," Roddy said. He had a crack in his voice that sounded like fear, until I realized he was playin' the elderly-man card, acting old and fragile. It was crafty and pathetic at the same time. "We don't want no trouble."

Steven ignored the ploy. "This ain't good, you guys. You're forcing my hand here."

"I'm sorry, Jinx," Shannon squeezed in. "Luna was an accident. He didn't mean—"

"Shut up, Shannon! You don't owe him an explanation."

"The hell she don't!" Roddy dropped the routine. Steven steadied his gun on him.

"Luna was in the wrong place at the wrong time. That's all there is to it. What she drank was meant for Charlie, not her." There was no conviction in his voice, no remorse.

"Wrong place at the wrong time? Why the hell are you givin' anybody poison in the first place, you asshole?" Roddy was beside himself at hearing Luna was indeed killed. I know we were both hoping there was no truth to any of it.

"If your woman lived here with this kind of trash, you'd see to it she was safe," Steven said.

"Safe? Safe from what? Some drunk beggin' for money? Safe from somebody catching a glimpse of tit through the window?"

"You don't know what they're capable of! Some of these guys are desperate. This place has all kinds of rats running through it. Hell, you had a drug dealer living here! I ain't lettin' my woman get struck by a stray bullet when a deal goes south."

Roddy was on a roll, so I let him keep the floor. "Okay, first of all, this little girl ain't no woman, ya pervert. Second, if you gave two shits about her, you'd provide a better place. Any real man would."

"He can't. He's married," she said.

"I said shut up, Shannon!" Steven yelled.

"And third, Mr. Toasty over there was dealin' weed, not cocaine. You watch too much TV, son."

Steven didn't like any of that and declared so by pulling back the hammer on his gun. Half a second later, I saw Charlie behind him, swinging his giant tea mug at the back of Steven's head. Steven's eyes bulged as the mug shattered, and he let out a little hiss through pursed lips, then kissed the floor with his teeth. I saw at least one tooth escape and hide under the bed. I was hoping he'd choke on the others. Either way, he didn't move.

It hadn't registered that the gun went off until I caught a glimpse of Roddy looking down at his leg. He was staring at a large hole in his prosthetic. Smoke billowed and splinters jutted. It was made of wood after all.

Shannon had already grabbed the gun and was pointing it at Charlie. She told him to get in the apartment, and he complied, though reluctantly, and a bit confused.

"I told you to stay away from here, Charlie. It's too dangerous. Why didn't you listen?" Shannon asked.

He threw up his hand, which still had the mug's handle gripped in a white-knuckled fist. "It's Tuesday."

I could have hugged the guy.

Shannon held the gun on all of us now, switching targets every so often, making sure we knew who was boss. Her hand shook like a junkie with a jackhammer. "I'm so sorry, Jinx. Luna really was an accident. I'm not even sure how it happened. I'm no murderer."

"Well, there's a few people not breathing anymore who would beg to differ."

"That's Steven's doing. He was just looking out for me. He didn't want me around dangerous people."

"But he'll let you stand on the street corner?" Roddy asked.

"I'm not a whore. I was pretending. I didn't want anyone asking where rent came from. Steven's married, and he's on probation…I didn't want anything linked to him."

"Why the hell not? The guy's an asshole." I said.

"Because he loves me and is looking out for me. He's going to leave his wife, and we're going to move away from here. He just needs to pick the right time to do it."

"He isn't looking out for anybody but himself, Shannon. I hate to say it, but this is textbook stuff right here. He's dragging you along while he keeps his marriage. You're just the piece on the side."

"Don't say that."

"He was killing people for crying out loud!" Roddy yelled.

"They were just people he thought were dangerous."

"You said that already, but I don't think you believe it. Homeless drunks? A stoner who didn't know his right from his left?"

"Steven made that list and gave it to me. He told me to stay away from those people. I didn't know his plans. I just know he's trying to do what's best for me...for us."

"You can't possibly believe any of that." I said.

"I...I don't know." She finally broke down and started crying. "I just know he has big plans for us."

"*Had*," Roddy said. "He ain't breathin'."

We all looked down at Steven and the spreading pool of red around him.

"I...I only hit him once," Charlie said. He was shaking pretty bad. "I was just trying to help."

"This ain't no movie. Sometimes once is enough," Roddy said.

Shannon bent down, put a hand on Steven's chest, kept the gun on us. She was quiet for a while, didn't panic, didn't scream. I think she was waking up, realizing this was a way out of something she should have left a long time ago.

"Call an ambulance." She said it calmly. "Wait...don't call. Give me your money. Both of you."

Roddy and I gave her what we had.

"You're making this a whole lot worse, little lady," Roddy said.

"I'm sorry. This isn't me, but I've got no choice. I can't go to jail. I'm leaving this place. I'm leaving this whole nasty city." She looked down at Steven. There was no mourning. I could tell it was bittersweet for her, and I think deep down she never believed a word the guy said. "Okay, I'm backing out of here. You're gonna give me your phones, and you're gonna give me fifteen minutes before you leave this room."

"I won't do that, Shannon. Like Roddy said, this isn't a movie."

She tightened her grip on the gun as she pointed it at me.

"People were killed. People who didn't deserve it. None of them did."

"I didn't kill them!"

"You were a part of it."

"I didn't know!" She held the gun out farther, closer to my face.

"You knew about Luna."

"That wasn't my fault!"

"You knew what Steven was capable of."

"It doesn't matter. I couldn't have stopped him," she cried. "You didn't know him."

I looked around the room. Charlie had taken a spot on the bed, mug handle still in hand. Roddy wore a look that could've shriveled a bull's nuts. He'd had enough, and I could tell he was about to speak. None of us wanted to die, but I think we all felt a little safer knowing the real danger was dead at our feet, and I didn't think Shannon had it in her to pull the trigger.

Apparently, Roddy felt the same because he said, "I'm leaving, young lady. That gun going off just about made me piss myself and I've got a bladder full of caffeine, so I'm gonna go empty it in my own toilet. And if you wanna stop me then you'll have to kill me, cuz ain't no teenaged troublemaker gonna make me piss my pants here in front of everyone. I've got my dignity, and I've been through rougher shit than this, so move outta the way or pull that trigger."

Roddy didn't wait for a response. He just charged forward and Shannon jumped out of the way, keeping the gun on him.

"If you're wanting to get any kind of headstart you'd better leave now," I told her.

She snatched her journal off the bed, ran out of the apartment and got into Steven's car, then pulled onto Sunset.

Chapter 27: The Lady in the Window

Roddy hadn't been lying about needing to pee. It's the first thing he did when he got out of there. Then he called the police. He never did call the ambulance.

I told Charlie it'd be a good idea if he stuck around, and not to worry, he did what he had to, and we'd testify to such. I made him some tea using his specific instructions, and filled him in on what had transpired within the past week. I even told him he was our number one suspect right up until earlier that day.

The police were there most of the afternoon, questioning folks, going through Shannon's apartment. They even brought the crime lab and scoured both hers and The Jeff's apartments. After the dust cleared, I offered my shower to Charlie. He teared up and told me he'd been waiting a lifetime for someone to offer. Roddy hooked him up with a couple of fresh shirts and some socks and underwear, but all his pants had either one leg hemmed at the thigh or cut off completely, so I gave him a pair of mine, along with my belt.

The next morning, Roddy and I ate at a little diner called *Connie's* that would become a regular spot for us. He snuck in a bottle of ranch for his eggs and toast, and we ate our usual breakfast. We'd found out Shannon had already gotten caught only 100 miles outside L.A. based on a tip I'd given the police. I remembered her talking about her half-brother in Santa Barbara. Sure enough, she'd headed straight there.

"You know," Roddy said with a mouthful of ranch toast. "I would've clocked that chick if it came down to it."

"She *did* have a gun."

"Yep. That's when anything goes, lady or not...speaking of ladies, who do we have here?" He pointed toward the diner windows where a gorgeous woman with a mile-wide smile stood tapping on the glass.

It was Audrey.

"That's her, ain't it?" Roddy asked.

"Sure is."

"I'm telling you, Jinx. A year from now you'll be on your honeymoon."

As I stood to greet Audrey, I could hear the sound of knuckles knocking on wood underneath the table.

About the Author:

Chad has written for Famous Monsters of Filmland, Rue Morgue, Cemetery Dance, and Scream magazine. He's had a few dozen short stories published, and some of his books include: OF FOSTER HOMES & FLIES, WALLFLOWER, STIRRING THE SHEETS, SKULLFACE BOY, THE SAME DEEP WATER AS YOU, THE PALE WHITE, and OUT BEHIND THE BARN co-written with John Boden. Lutzke's work has been praised by authors Jack Ketchum, Richard Chizmar, Stephen Graham Jones, James Newman, Elizabeth Massie, and his own mother. He can be found lurking the internet at www.chadlutzke.com

I Believe in Gratitude:

Thank you to the following people for either their direct help or inspiration regarding The Neon Owl: My wife, Mary Lutzke, John Boden, Bob Ford, Jim Rockford, Joe Lansdale, Jonathan Ames, Sean Baker, Bobby, David Lynch, Matt Hayward, Lydia Capuano, Sterp, Patrick Freivald, Rich Duncan, Laurel Hightower. And of course to my patrons who were with me every step of the way: Connie McNeil Bracke, Shannon Everyday, Steve Gracin, Shaun Hupp, Michael Perez, Tim Feely, Dyane Hendershot, George Ranson, Liane Abe, Steven Gomzi, Dean Watts, Karlee Stranger Dream, Mindi Snyder, Diamond Kennedy, Shannan Ross, Wayne Fenlon, Tracy Robinson, Jamie Goecker, Cassie Daley, Vitina Molgaard, John Questore, Edward Lorn, Scott Kemper, Kimberly Napolitano, Jacqueline Boyster, Jenny DelDuca, Robert Dabicci, Melissa Potter, Kevin Whitten, Michael Fowler, Christian Berntsen, Remo MaCartney, Todd Keisling, Jerri Nall, Barbara Haynes, Danielle Milton, Shannon Bradner, Alex Pearson, Beth Lee, Kim Hastings, Mary Kiefel, Jason White, Brennan LaFaro, Alyssa Manning, Linsey, Josh Edwards, Kurt Boylstein, Dirk Gard, Rachel, William Proctor, Stephanie Briggs, Lee-ann Oleski, and Karen Moore.

Other books written by Chad Lutzke:
Of Foster Homes & Flies
Wallflower
Stirring the Sheets
Skullface Boy
Out Behind the Barn (co-written with John Boden)
The Same Deep Water as You
The Pale White

Collections:
Night as a Catalyst
Spicy Constellation & Other Recipes

To join my VIP reader list and be included in all future giveaways, visit www.chadlutzke.com
To become a patron and receive exclusive content and benefits, visit
www.patreon.com/ChadLutzke

Made in the USA
Middletown, DE
07 October 2023

40405925R00102